The Murder Convention

All the titles in The Blind Sleuth Mysteries:

1943: D for Daisy

1946: First Spring in Paris

1952: Honeymoon in Rio

1956: Cockett's Last Cock-up

1960: Murder on the High Sea

1964: The Desiderata Stone

1967: Blind Angel of Wrath

1972: Berlin Fall

1984: The Nightlife of the Blind

1986: Daisy's Pushkin Duel

1989: Daisy and Bernard

1992: The Desiderata Gold

AD 67: The Desiderata Riddle

AD 76: Desiderata's Lost Cause

1990s: Back to Africa

1990s: The Icarus Case

AD 79: August in Pompeii

1990s: The Murder Convention

1990s: The Empty Grave Chronicles

AD 87: The Ghost Player

Nick Aaron

The Murder
Convention

A Blind Sleuth Mystery

ANOTHER IMPRINT PUBLISHERS

Belgian legal deposit D/2024/Nicolaas Jan Ouwehand, publisher
ISBN 9789083433837

Their feet run to evil, they make haste to shed blood. You can't catch a bird that saw you spanning your net, yet these people ambush themselves and lie in wait for their own destruction. For such is the fate of all who pursue gain dishonestly: it robs those who profit from it of their lives.

Proverbs 1:16-19

Contents

I Murder is more than a corpse on the floor

— 1 —

It all started when Daisy ordered a massage table. She wanted to set it up in the guestroom. There was only one bed there, a dresser and a nightstand, so there would be plenty of space to fit in the contraption. There was even a washbasin with cold and hot water, which seemed ideal. The only problem was that Darren wouldn't have much room for his wheelchair, but as he said himself, he could live with that, he had no business being there anyway. As long as she gave him massages in their own bedroom and helped him keep his paralysed legs fit he would be all right.

The fact was that Daisy missed her old job, and longed to take up physiotherapy again, to treat other patients, apart from Darren. With all the ailments she encountered on a daily basis at the Manor Hotel, and with a lifetime of healing power at her fingertips, there was no retiring from practice after all. Living on the attic floor of a fancy hotel, you got to know a lot of people, women mostly, who had to work long hours for a pittance: cleaners, chambermaids, waitresses, kitchen hands and the like. They worked hard, and even though they didn't like to complain as a rule, Daisy had sometimes overheard some of them muttering among themselves: "My back is killing me... my legs feel like logs." She couldn't help herself and had offered her assistance.

The first therapy sessions had been improvised on unused beds in vacant rooms, but they'd been a great success regardless, especially when this strange angel of mercy had scoffed at the very idea of getting paid for her spontaneous services. "If you're feeling better, my dear, that's the only reward I want."

And feel better her new patients did. They spread the word, and before she knew it Daisy had to start thinking about a professional massage table for the sake of her own back. And a dedicated practice space in the guest room. The 'girls' absolutely loved it. The simple fact of being allowed inside the mysterious loft apartment on the top floor of their place of work was thrilling enough, but the blind old lady who lived there was so *nice* to them, and her treatments really worked. She became rather busy during the staff's lunch breaks and at the end of their shifts. She told Darren that the two of them simply needed to adapt their routine a bit, taking their morning strolls slightly earlier and things like that. It was not a problem, he replied, he was happy if she was.

"Thank you for being so sweet... It won't stay this busy forever, I hope, once the treatments start working."

And that is how Daisy befriended quite a number of young women, most of them with rather exotic names such as Tatyana, Agnieszka or Ilona, the menial jobs clearly no longer held by 'local girls'. Some of her patients had strong Slavic accents, but it didn't keep them from sharing the latest gossip with their benefactress while she was treating their sore muscles and stiff joints. Daisy was learning inte-

10

resting things every day about the running of a fancy hotel. The receptionist, in particular, who had a backache from sitting at her desk for hours, worked with a computer. Her name was Sondra.

"A *computer!* How impressive! We had one too at my last group practice, but it always remained a great mystery to me. I could blind-type on a qwerty keyboard all right, but I had no idea *where* my typing went. I missed *feeling* my way around a piece of paper, you know?"

"Yes, I can imagine."

"And *Sondra*, what kind of name is that? Why not *Sandra*? What is it with you modern girls, having such fancy names as Kiyana, Jayden or Shanise, if I may ask?"

Sondra chortled long and hard. "You *really* have no idea, don't you? It's because we're... um... from Jamaica, although I was born in Hackney myself, but you see what I mean."

"You mean you're, like, *black* or something?"

"Bless you, Daisy, you've got it in one! This is really priceless, I can't wait to tell the others. I suppose it's an unexpected bonus of being blind, that, you know?"

"Yes, I like to think there's a lot more to blindness than merely not seeing."

Anyway, it was from Sondra, while she was soothing her backache, that Daisy heard that 'The Murder Convention' was scheduled to be held at the Manor Hotel. Her patient herself had booked the reservations on her computer.

"Well, to start with I had a phone call from the personal assistant of the famous mystery writer Theodora Slayer."

"Never heard of her."

"But she's a best-selling author! Even I know that, although I'm not much of a reader. And I would have thought that *you* must *love* murder mysteries."

"Oh no, not if they're made up... I'm only interested in *real-life* murders."

Anyway, the famous writer's PA wanted to book *ten* rooms for *ten* days, and asked Sondra if and when the Manor Hotel could accommodate such a group. She explained that the ten prospective guests would all be mystery writers, belonging to an informal little club that dubbed themselves 'The Top Ten', being the top-ten best-selling authors of murder mysteries on the British market. Once in a while they came together on a fancy location, preferably out of season when the fares were low, in order to bond, exchange experiences, and possibly write a joint chronicle of the proceedings, something light-hearted, mind you, nothing serious, just for the fun of it. They held such a gathering every two or three years, depending, and when it finally took place they called it The Murder Convention. Sondra searched in her computer and spotted a slot at the end of November, when the hotel could provide ten single rooms for even longer than ten days if necessary. "In fact, if you book at that time, you'll probably be our *only* guests for the duration."

"Well that sounds ideal," Mrs Slayer's PA had replied. Then she'd asked Sondra: was the establishment really an old-fashioned *country house?* Did it have a library, for instance? Did the library have a *fireplace* and was it possible to actually light a fire there to create a cosy atmosphere for the members of the club? Yes, yes, the receptionist assured her, in November they could have a fire in the library all right, no worries. And the hotel, while completely refurbished to modern standards, was an authentic *old pile.* It used to be called 'Bottomleigh House', the seat of the Earls of Haverford, no less. In fact, the last dowager Countess of that name was still in residence.

"That would be you, Daisy. Mister Robbins instructed us to mention this at every opportunity, I hope you don't mind."

"Not at all," the physiotherapist tittered, still massaging her patient on the brand-new treatment table in her guestroom, "anything to be of assistance."

Anyway, before she finalised the booking, the PA on the phone started pestering Sondra about all kinds of practical details. Did the rooms have en-suite bath, shower, and WC facilities? Did the chef who prepared the meals have any verifiable references? Did the hotel have an indoor pool? On that last point the receptionist had to disappoint her 'prospect': there was an *outdoor* pool on the garden terrace, but it was emptied in the fall. No gym either, no. As available physical activity she could only suggest walks on the beautiful property surrounding the hotel, or in the countryside beyond. There even was a pretty pond on the grounds.

"I ask you, Daisy, people want an authentic manor house, but they're miffed if it doesn't have an indoor pool!"

"I know, people are strange, sometimes."

"Anyway, what clinched the deal in the end, you'll never guess… was my *computer!* I happened to mention it, and the woman asked if I would be able to do some typing on it and print out ten copies of each document for the participants. You see, Theodora Slayer's PA has a computer too."

So the ten 'singles' were booked for the end of November—just around Daisy's birthday, as chance would have it. Sondra was expected to type up, print and distribute all the documents related to The Murder Convention, including a daily bulletin of the 'proceedings'.

"I already have a list of the ten participants in my computer, and the questionnaire they will receive when they arrive. It's very tongue-in-cheek, clearly designed for them to display their literary prowess… If you're interested I can give you a copy of both. I mean, you obviously can't *read* them yourself, but I guess your husband can."

"Yes, Darren will certainly do that for me, and I *am* interested… This convention seems to have a pretty impressive potential for causing trouble."

"I *knew* you'd be interested!" Sondra chuckled.

— 2 —

Daisy's new friend was true to her word. Two documents in an unsealed envelope were dropped in her letterbox before the next post was delivered. When Darren described the mysterious letter, marked only "For Daisy", his wife smiled, and exclaimed, "That's from Sondra, from reception downstairs. Open it, quick!" And it were indeed a list of names and a questionnaire, both produced on a computer, looking as if they'd come straight from the local printers. Such wonders of modern technology were lost on poor Daisy, but she found them quite fascinating nevertheless.

The list of participants, for instance, was drawn up in alphabetical order of surnames, and she knew that a computer could sort out any number of items in a given 'file' at the flip of a switch, as it were. Therefore the prospective guests were listed as: James Adam; Jim Cross; John Drew; Jessica Holmes; Aggie Maple; Lee Quincy; Jack Reaper; Anthony Saccharine; Theodora T Slayer; Ruth Vine. She and Darren didn't know any of them, except that Daisy had heard the name Theodora Slayer from Sondra. But then again, if you didn't like reading mysteries particularly and couldn't be bothered to keep up with even the most successful authors of the day, you were bound to have missed these ten authors, best-selling though they might be.

Darren had parked his chair right next to where his wife had seated herself, at the end of an upholstered bench, without armrests, that they'd bought especially so they could sit close together. He extracted a second piece of paper from the envelope, also neatly printed, and proceeded to read it aloud for his wife.

Ten questions for the participants
of the Top Ten Club's Murder Convention

Dear colleagues and nevertheless friends,

Maybe this time around we'll finally manage to realise our old ambition of at least *starting* to write a collaborative novel at our periodical gathering. The ten questions I submit to you are clearly designed as a warming-up to that end. Take your time and give them your best.

Yours sincerely, Theodora T Slayer

1) If you were going to murder someone during our convention, which one of us would it be? Don't be coy, one of your beloved colleagues is going to mark you as a prospective *victim* too, you know.

2) If someone were murdered during our convention, which participant would be your *prime suspect*, and why? Again, don't be coy, one of us is bound to finger you in return.

3) If you murdered someone, anyone, during our convention, what would your *motive* be? Please don't state the obvious, that you would gladly kill for a best-seller right now.

4) If a murder were committed during our convention, we expect that all of you would have a watertight *alibi*. What would be yours? Who do you think would come up with the most original one, and what would that be?

5) If you had to come up with the perfect crime, what *modus operandi* would you devise to kill one of your fellow-participants? How would you create the *opportunity* and find the *means* for an unsolvable murder?

6) The best way to cover up your crime would be to make it look like someone else did it. Which one of your beloved colleagues would you frame for murder, as a *red herring* to put the police off the scent?

7) Obviously you would be the best *sleuth* to solve a murder, if such took place during our convention. But to which other participant would you rather entrust the investigation if you'd been murdered, and why?

8) What would be your weapon of choice in the event, you've already guessed it, that you'd want to kill somebody? And which *murder weapons* would you ascribe to your colleagues? Make a list, if you can.

9) What would be the best *time and place* for a hypothetical murder during our little gathering? Please don't state the obvious by answering 'In the middle of the night in the old manor's library'.

10) Naturally *you* wouldn't leave any *clues* if you committed a murder, but your colleagues certainly would. Which clues would each one of them be most likely to leave behind on the crime scene? Please make a list.

Daisy thanked her husband and patted his arm, "You're getting really good at this, darling, beautiful intonation and all that."

Then she marvelled, "Well-well-well... The first thing I said to Sondra when she told me about this 'Murder Convention' was that it seemed to have a pretty impressive potential for causing trouble. Now the famous 'questionnaire' only confirms my impression. What a *number* this Theodora Slayer must be! Why not just say it plainly: 'I'm counting on one of you to *murder* one of the others'? Phew!"

"Do you *disapprove*, precious?"

"*Of course* I disapprove! Murder is a serious matter. I just don't understand how people can make a joke out of it, or at least the subject of light-hearted banter, like it's just some kind of *entertainment* or something."

"Well, you could argue that it's not so bad to fantasise about it, rather than to be fascinated by the real thing like you are. I'm just saying."

"Well don't. I've never *encouraged* anyone, you know. It's just that I seem to attract these kinds of... *mishaps* like a

16

magnet, and that I'm damn good at solving them."

"Well, wouldn't it be an idea to start *writing* about them instead of attracting them? It would be a lot less stressful all around... I even wouldn't mind doing the typing for you if you buy us a computer."

"I don't know, darling, the idea just doesn't appeal. For now, let's go for a walk on the grounds."

It was when they came back from their stroll an hour later that they were ambushed by Mister Robbins, the hotel's manager. They were crossing the old manor's monumental entrance hall, currently the lobby where Sondra officiated behind the reception desk, and he intercepted them just as they made for the lift. He stopped them in their tracks.

"Mrs Hayes... Mr Miller, could I have a word, please?"

"A good afternoon to you too, Robbins. Are you going to complain again about Darren leaving tyre marks in the carpeting?"

"No, this time my grievance is with you, Mrs Hayes, if I may be so bold. It has come to my knowledge that you've been providing physical therapy to some of my employees."

"Have you been *spying* on me?"

"Not at all, but you do understand that I can't allow you to use my establishment's premises to set up a practice and do business on the sly... without even notifying me. What you're doing is probably completely illegal."

"Rubbish! Utter balderdash! I can show you my diplomas... or rather, why should I? I have the right to do as I please in my own home, so it's none of your business."

"Well, speaking about business, have you registered your practice with the proper authorities? Are you paying the mandatory taxes on the revenue it generates? Am I wrong to strongly doubt it?"

"Yes, you certainly are, Robbins, for the simple reason

that I'm providing my services free of charge... naturally. I wouldn't *dream* of billing your employees, who couldn't afford to pay for my services anyway. The poor girls work themselves to death for a pittance, as you well know."

"My employees make the mandatory working hours and receive the hospitality industry's standard salaries..."

"My point exactly: when they need therapy they hardly have the time nor the resources to seek help. Be glad that I can treat them during their lunch breaks or after hours, so they don't need to go on sick leave."

"My only objection is that you're inflicting unfair competition on those therapists who *do* run a bona fide business and try to make an honest living from it."

"Well, thanks for reminding me why I should never, ever, offer a free massage to any of the paying guests!"

"You'll never admit that I could be right and you could be wrong about anything, would you ever, Mrs Hayes?"

"You're damn right about that, Mister Robbins... Oh but wait, I just did, didn't I?"

When the manager finally gave up and slunk off, shaking his head and snorting with frustration, Daisy proceeded again in the general direction of the lift, pushing her husband's wheelchair, and growled under her breath: "That man! I could kill him!"

Darren, and Sondra, who'd heard everything from behind the reception desk, both tutted indulgently.

— 3 —

One by one the guests arrived. From their attic flat Daisy could hear the scrunching of tyres on the front court's gravel outside, and Darren, peeping down through the banister of their roof loggia, would identify and describe the type and

18

make of the posh automobiles that conveyed the prosperous-looking participants to the locale of the Murder Convention. Normally the two couldn't care less whether the hotel was fully booked or almost empty, the comings and goings varied with the seasons and barely registered with them, but this was something else entirely. They had to admit it: they were losing their cool.

So each time a guest disembarked from a fancy conveyance, Daisy and Darren made up an excuse, any excuse, to go down at once, and just 'happened' to be crossing the hall at the same moment the newcomer approached the reception desk after supervising the safe unloading and carrying inside of a ton of luxurious-looking luggage. As Daisy explained to Darren, "If they notice our presence when they arrive, it will make things a lot easier later on." And why wouldn't they notice them? The elderly lady's round dark glasses clearly spelled that she was totally blind, and the much younger man in the wheelchair was strikingly handsome, with a beard and long hair that made him look like Jesus Christ. So it worked like a charm. In fact, when Theodora Slayer saw them, she stepped over at once and introduced herself, before asking boldly: "Are you the Dowager Countess of Haverford, by any chance, Milady?"

"Yes, I am that, when necessary. But please, Mrs Slayer, just call me Daisy."

"Only if you call me Thea, my dear. Delighted to meet you, I'm sure we'll talk again and I look forward to it."

And then she bustled off again. Obviously her PA had blabbed, rather, after her telephone conversation with Sondra.

The manager was also there, obsequiously supervising each new arrival in turn, and he didn't like the competition. At some point he couldn't help himself, he stepped over to

Daisy and Darren as soon as yet another guest had disappeared inside the lift, and he hissed with exasperated urgency, "May I ask what you're doing here, *again*, Mrs Hayes?"

"Just passing through, Robbins, a sheer coincidence."

"But you're there *each time* a guest arrives!"

"Oh well, the dowager countess likes to mingle with the *hoi polloi*, don't you know?"

And the beleaguered man was in for even more trials, as the resident couple from the attic loft chose that same day to dine in the hotel's restaurant. They hardly ever did this, and he was glad they didn't, officially because the paying guests were entitled to a table, and it was not always convenient to cater to unexpected 'external' eaters. Although he also found the presence of a bumbling blind woman—with a much younger wheelchair-bound husband in tow—deeply embarrassing for his establishment. Daisy and Darren were aware of this and rather put off, as a rule. You know when you're not wanted. But on that day they overcame their misgivings and 'went down' for dinner: with only ten guests there would be plenty of room for two more, and they were just too curious to meet the newcomers.

It was a great success. The mystery writers were all there, sitting around the three largest tables in groups of three or four. When 'the Countess' and 'Jesus Christ' entered the room, Theodora Slayer immediately left her table to 'welcome them in their midst', and graciously invited them to sit with her at a fourth table. They were still having cocktails, she said, not too late to change settings. Then a younger man, who introduced himself as Jack Reaper, joined them, "To make the table complete, two ladies and two gentlemen, you know."

"Very good, Jack," the older writer retorted, "at least you have good manners, in spite of it all."

"What's *that* supposed to mean, my dear Thea?"

"Well, my young colleague here," Thea explained to Daisy in a mock-confidential tone, "is an upcoming author of best-sellers, who's been invited for the first time, which should fill him with gratitude, but I'm afraid we of the old school—'the dinosaurs of crime fiction'—are not much to his liking."

"That just isn't true, I'm delighted to be here."

"I'm only quoting your own words, Jack. You called us that in your most recent interview."

"Oh, you of all people should know how it is, my dear, one tends to make brash pronouncements in front of journalists. You've produced some pretty strong quotes yourself in your time... famously so."

"Well, as you can hear my dear Daisy, we're a lively bunch, you and your husband will have to make allowances."

"Oh, we will, we're great fans of you all, we're completely star-struck."

The two writers clucked contentedly, and the older lady announced that she would make sure they were introduced to all of them. "It's going to be a long evening, as we have nothing else to do for the moment, so if you care to stick around..."

She added that writing is a lonely profession, that therefore the presence of a couple of fans was only a bonus, and that they were welcome to join the company whenever they wanted. "We like to have an audience to witness our shenanigans, you know? It's a pity, in that respect, that this hotel is almost *deserted* right now, I would have preferred to have some more... *public* around. I blame my PA for this."

Daisy smiled, and didn't mention that the PA had clearly been looking for a *cheap* arrangement, rather than a full hotel. But she wasn't supposed to know about this. In the end the evening turned out to be very fruitful. As she'd mapped the list of participants in her mind, she could easily pretend to be familiar with their names, and to be a great fan of each one of them in turn while she and Darren were led around from one table to the next by their hostess.

"Aggie? You must be Agatha Maple, I've heard so much about you! What are you writing right now? Please tell me all about it!"

And Darren just tagged along, not saying much, but observing the proceedings and fulfilling his usual role of being his blind wife's eyes. Later he would have to describe all these people in detail to her, fill her in on the visual clues to their character: clothing, grooming, facial expressions and body language. He had become quite proficient at this, and besides, he never forgot a face. And he told anyone who would engage him in conversation, "You have to watch your step with my darling wife, you know. She's not only a great fan, she's also a real wannabe. Her fondest dream is to become a mystery writer herself, and before you know it she might become part of the competition!"

The next day, on the second day of the convention, the participants were kept busy answering their questionnaires to the best of their abilities, that is to say as wittily and originally as possible. Nevertheless the club convened in the dining room for breakfast and lunch, and in the library for their morning coffee and afternoon tea. Daisy made sure she was present too, and as the guests liked to take strolls on the grounds in between bouts of sparkling writing, she and Darren patrolled the park as well, making themselves available for friendly chats. By the end of that first full day she'd managed to get a clearer picture of them all, and when everyone retired to their own quarters before dinner she was able to draw up a list of their profiles, banging away on her faithful Perkin Brailler, just for the fun of it. Then it was her turn to read out loud to Darren.

The ten participants of
the Top Ten Club's Murder Convention

Theodora T Slayer (Thea) is a successful but rather old-school author, who prides herself on having sold more books than any of the other participants, but that is due to the fact that she's been very prolific for a long time, producing one novel a year since the early 50s. She's a present-day proponent of the Agatha Christie tradition of puzzle-like and fair-play mysteries.

She's the one who organizes these conventions (with a little help from her long-suffering PA) and clearly sees herself as in charge of the proceedings. She doesn't suffer fools gladly, has a dominant personality and tends to be a bit overbearing sometimes. She struggles to hide her sense of superiority and her disregard for her colleagues, whom she considers rather worthless compared to herself. Everybody dislikes her for that but no one dares to show it.

She's at the top of the list of candidates to be murdered.

Jack Reaper is a young and upcoming best-selling author, second only to Thea in terms of annual sales since his last book's resounding success.

In recent interviews in the national press he didn't hide his dislike and contempt for 'the old crocodiles', thereby referring to all the mystery writers who are older than he is, which most of them are by a wide margin. But now that he has been invited to the convention for the first time, he carefully avoids such abrasive remarks and clearly strives to ingratiate himself with his colleagues.

The question is whether they are being taken in.

Ruth Vine is a middle-aged, demure lady author. Not very successful compared to the two above, but generally respected for the literary quality of her work. Rumour has it that she's Thea's niece, and as her famous aunt is childless she and a few cousins stand to inherit quite a fortune in the event of her death. (Slayer is not the aunt's real surname, but Ruth Vine is really Ruth Vine, by the way.)

Just for the fun of it: could this be another motive for murder?

AGATHA MAPLE (AGGIE) IS AN ATTRACTIVE YOUNG THING—THE ONLY ONE ACTUALLY YOUNGER THAN JACK REAPER—WHO IS VERY SUCCESSFUL WITH LITTLE NOVELS WHERE SPICY SEXUAL INTRIGUES LEAD TO MURDERS, THAT IN THEIR TURN REQUIRE A LOT OF SLEEPING AROUND BY A WELL-BUILT HUNK OF A DETECTIVE FOR THEIR SOLUTION.

AGGIE HERSELF IS FOLLOWED BY A TRAIL OF SEXUAL INTRIGUE WHEREVER SHE GOES, ESPECIALLY WHEN THERE ARE SEVERAL UNATTACHED MALES (FOR THE DURATION OF A CONVENTION, FOR EXAMPLE) IN THE PICTURE.

SHE MAY NOT BECOME THE VICTIM OF A MURDER, BUT COULD CERTAINLY CAUSE ONE.

JOHN DREW WRITES LEGAL THRILLERS AND IS QUITE THE EXPERT ON POLICE AND LEGAL PROCEDURES. HE HAS AN ANNOYING TENDENCY TO PESTER HIS COLLEAGUES ABOUT ALL KINDS OF PETTY DETAILS THEY ALLEGEDLY 'GOT COMPLETELY WRONG' IN THEIR OWN NOVELS, WHICH DOESN'T MAKE HIM POPULAR WITH THE REST OF THE CLUB.

NOT A MOTIVE FOR MURDER, PERHAPS, BUT SOME WOULD LIKE TO THROTTLE HIM.

JIM CROSS IS A GOOD-LOOKING AND ELEGANT MAN WHOSE WHODUNNITS ARE BASED ON A JAMES-BOND-LIKE ADVENTURER-CUM-PRIVATE-EYE. HE IS QUITE FAMOUS AS A MAN-ABOUT-TOWN AND A WOMANIZER. RUMOUR HAS IT THAT HE RELENTLESSLY PURSUES YOUNG AGGIE AT EVERY OPPORTUNITY, WITHOUT ANY SUCCESS SO FAR.

IS THE STAGE SET FOR A STEAMY CRIME PASSIONNEL?

ANTHONY SACCHARINE HAS BASED HIS CONSIDERABLE SUCCESS ON THE GENRE OF THE FORENSIC MYSTERY. HE KNOWS EVERYTHING ABOUT THE MATERIAL EVIDENCE SURROUNDING CRIMES AND MISDEMEANOURS. IN CONVERSATION HE CAN TICK OFF HALF A DOZEN WAYS OF DISPATCHING A PERSON WITHOUT LEAVING A TRACE. A FASCINATING MAN TO TALK TO, THEREFORE.

IF ANYONE DIES 'MYSTERIOUSLY' WE'LL KNOW WHOM TO SUSPECT.

JESSICA HOLMES WRITES COSY MYSTERIES ABOUT A CUPCAKE BAKERY WHERE CORPSES TURN UP ON A DAILY BASIS AND THE CAT SOLVES THE MURDER MYSTERY EVERY TIME. THE GREATEST MYSTERY IS HOW YOU END UP ON THE BEST-SELLER LISTS WITH SUCH TRIPE, EVERYONE ELSE WONDERS.

JESSICA WOULD CERTAINLY LIKE TO THROTTLE A FEW PEOPLE, IF ONLY SHE COULD KEEP IT HIDDEN FROM THE CAT.

JAMES ADAM WRITES ABOUT A BUMBLING POLICE DETECTIVE WHO SOLVES CRIMES WITHOUT EVEN TRYING. BUT HE KEEPS REPEATING THAT YOU DON'T END UP IN THE TOP TEN WITHOUT EVEN TRYING.

IF HE SHOULD KILL ANYONE, HE WOULD PROBABLY JUST STUMBLE INTO IT.

LEE QUINCY WRITES ABOUT A HISTORICAL PRIVATE EYE IN ANCIENT ROME NAMED PHILIPPUS MARLOVIUS. EVERYONE IS IMPRESSED BY HIS KNOWLEDGE OF HISTORY, IF NOT BY ANYTHING ELSE. LIKE THE TWO OTHER 'SPECIALISTS' ABOVE, HE IS QUITE SUCCESSFUL, BUT ENJOYS PRECIOUS LITTLE RESPECT FROM HIS PEERS.

COULD LACK OF APPRECIATION BE A MOTIVE FOR MURDER?

"You're quite enjoying this, huh?" Darren teased after his wife had finished reading.

"Well, up to a point. You heard what I said to Sondra, just a while ago."

On their way to the elevator they'd been hailed by the receptionist, who'd told them that she was busy typing out the answers to the questionnaire from all the participants, and she'd asked Daisy if she wanted her to print some extra copies for her.

"*Ten* times the jocular fantasies of a bunch of scribblers? Thank you but no, dear Sondra, I think I can already guess what they've come up with. There are more than enough murder scenarios that could be concocted in that group, with motives ranging from greed to revenge, by way of jealousy and sexual frustration. So I'll just stick to my own imaginings."

And that was exactly what she'd proceeded to do on the Perkin Brailler.

"But still, my precious," Darren insisted, "I wonder if you're not pining to become an author of mysteries yourself?"

"Well, let me put it this way, darling: I really *enjoy* talking to these people, you know? because they're all so intelligent and articulate... They're *writers*."

25

Daisy and Darren didn't get to hear 'the scream' that night. They slept right through it. Their attic flat was just too far removed from the rest of the hotel, and well-isolated.

But this did not apply for the rest of the company. The whole setup of Bottomleigh House made it impossible to ignore what was going on anywhere on the ground floor from anywhere upstairs. That had always been the whole point of these old country houses. With its monumental central staircase connecting the towering hall with the two landings above, it was quite easy to follow all the activity in the rest of the house if you just left the door of your room ajar. When new guests arrived for a house party, for instance, you heard them debarking in the hall, and you went down to greet them if you so wished. Likewise, when the huge oriental gong on the first landing was struck for lunch or supper, everybody knew at once to prepare themselves to repair to the dining room. The gong was still used in the Manor Hotel for its nostalgic thrill. But what all the participants of the Murder Convention heard that night was something else altogether.

A blood-curdling, endlessly drawn-out scream coming from downstairs.

Within seconds the first guests appeared at the staircase bannisters, still tying the waistbands of their dressing gowns. They peered down into the hall, glanced at one another, and exclaimed, "What was that? Did you hear that? What's going on?"

James Adam, the bumbling detective, who was friendly with the night porter, called down, "Mister Kumar, what's going on?"

"Oh... erm... I don't know, Sir, something ominous must have transpired, in the library, I think it is."

"Can't you go and have a look?"

"Oh no, Sir, I must stay behind at the reception desk, I'm not armed, you see."

Jim Cross, always striving to emulate his hero James Bond, looked at the others and grumbled, "That old fool is useless, we must go and check it out ourselves. Let's all go down together." He was eager to take action, even to lead the way, but not on his own if he could avoid it.

So, within a minute it was a whole group of mystery writers, including a couple of ladies, Ruth Vine and Jessica Holmes, that shuffled down the stairs and landed in the hall. "To the library, over there!" the square-jawed Jim Cross commanded, and strangely enough Mister Kumar too came out from behind the reception desk and followed them towards the monumental door, his curiosity now stronger than his pernickety sense of duty.

When Jim turned the handle, in fact an old-fashioned brass knob, he half-expected the door to be locked, so he pushed hard, but it was not, and it flew open rather dramatically. The huge library hall suddenly revealed itself, flooded in electric light. And empty. While Jim stood frozen on the threshold, the others tried to push him aside and looked past him, craning their necks. Then it was Ruth Vine who exclaimed, "Oh, look! blood on the rug!"

They took a few tentative steps inside, still jostling, Mister Kumar pushing from behind, raising himself on the tip of his toes.

"Don't touch anything!" John the procedural expert admonished them.

"Oh, shut up, Drew!" 'Bumbling James' grumbled, "this is not a crime scene investigation yet."

"Besides, that's more *my* speciality," Anthony Saccharine remarked, "but the first question that occurs to *me* is: if there's blood on the rug, where's the corpse?"

"There *is* no corpse, you fool," Jim Cross grumbled, "for the simple reason that no murder has taken place here! It stands to reason that this whole thing has been staged for our benefit. If there had been a murder, how could the culprit *possibly* get rid of the body in *two* minutes flat?"

"You're right," Anthony agreed, "not to mention producing so many blood splatters as well. It has every appearance that the blood was sprinkled on the carpet *before* the scream was produced."

"Oh, look!" Mister Kumar then exclaimed, "on the chimney mantelpiece! One of the big silver candlesticks is missing! Could it be the murder weapon, one wonders?"

He'd clearly not followed the guests' conversation closely, and therefore the others just ignored him.

"What was that? Did you hear that scream? What's going on here?"

Mister Robbins had suddenly appeared on the scene, not particularly up to date either, not unlike his employee, but he had the advantage over his guests of being fully dressed, therefore looking very much in charge. While the others were trying to make up their minds about just ignoring him as well, the demure Ruth Vine couldn't help herself and spoke up respectfully, as he was the hotel's manager after all.

"It's nothing to be alarmed about, sir, although I'm afraid someone has grievously fouled up one of your lovely rugs... with blood."

"The question is," Jim Cross added, "who did it? That's what I would like to know."

"Well, it can't be anyone of those who are here," John Drew pointed out, "as we all came down together only a minute after we heard the scream."

"Yes, but... the scream!" Robbins spluttered, "and what's this about blood? *Whose* blood?"

He pushed his way past the others, who were still congregated by the door, keeping a respectful distance from the ghastly red stains on the largest and most precious Persian rug in the middle of the library. He stepped over to the scene of the crime, knelt down by the offending stains, and started yammering, "Who could *do* such a thing?"

"My point exactly," Jim Cross said, and Ruth Vine added, "Someone's going to be in *biiig* trouble," while John Drew repeated, "Don't touch anything!"

Robbins righted himself again and strode back to the group by the door, looking accusingly at each one in turn. "How can you people stay so *calm?* How can you be so sure that no one was *murdered?* Didn't you hear the *scream?*"

Anthony Saccharine volunteered, "My dear Robbins, we've already concluded that the scream is neither here nor there. It seems that the blood *must* have been poured on the rug *before* that."

"If we want to find out for sure if anyone was murdered or not," John the 'proceduralist' added, "it's quite simple, really, we'll just have to check if anyone is *missing.*"

All the members of the group by the door started staring at those around them and made a mental tally.

"Dear Thea is not here, for one, slept right through the whole thing," someone reported.

"Same for Lee Quincy," another said, "sleeping like a Roman baby!"

"Where's Aggie?" Jim Cross asked, "Oh there you are, my dear, I hadn't spotted you yet."

"Erm, hello, I just arrived. What's going on?"

"Then there's Jack Reaper still missing," John Drew said, "and the couple from the attic too, the Countess and Jesus Christ."

"Let's go check on all of them!" Jim Cross exclaimed with manly determination, "we have to find out if anyone is *really* missing."

Just at that moment the outside doorbell rang, the night porter hurried back to his post behind the reception desk, activated the buzzer of the electric lock, and promptly the glass panes of the hotel's main entrance slid open in front of the assembled guests. Lee Quincy stumbled into the hotel lobby.

"Have I missed something?" he slurred, clearly a bit inebriated, "there seems to be quite a party going on here!"

"Quincy! Where have you been?" one of his colleagues demanded, "it's almost two in the morning!"

"Oh, I just had a night out, you know. You wouldn't credit it, but The Fly and Fish on the Horsham road is quite the place!"

"Have you been *driving* in that state?"

"So what if I have? The roads are empty at this hour anyway."

"Well, that accounts for one missing person, at least," Jim said, "now there are only two left, and the couple from the loft."

With great unity of purpose the whole group of guests set off towards the staircase, with the exception of Quincy, who just stood there, swaying, and wearily eying Mister Robbins and Mister Kumar, who eyed him back.

That is when Daisy and Darren finally heard about 'the scream'.

The telephone rang. Daisy got out of bed to pick it up. It was Mister Kumar, whom she didn't know well, because she and Darren hardly ever went out at night. He told her that he was calling from the reception desk and that "something ominous had transpired in the library"; he asked respectfully if she could come downstairs, preferably with her husband, as the guests of the hotel wished "to tally the occupants of the premises in order to ascertain if anyone was missing."

"Very well, Mister Kumar, Darren and I will come down in a moment."

Daisy was a bit puzzled by this request, but was curious as well—rather than anxious—about this "ominous something" going on in the middle of the night. She told Darren about it, and he exclaimed "Let's find out!" wide awake already.

The reason why the night porter had phoned was simple. While the guests wandered off to inspect the upper floors, knocking on doors, he'd realized at once that they wouldn't know how to get to the attic. Normally you had to take the lift, whose door opened straight into the flat's main room, but only if you had a special key. Visitors from outside needed to ring the bell at a back door and could access the lift from there when it was sent down. So Mister Kumar had decided that the simplest thing to do, at this impossible hour, was to ask the 'permanent residents' to come down themselves.

Anyway, by the time Daisy and Darren made their appearance in the lobby, both in dressing gowns, the guests had finished their inspection tour and were just coming downstairs to report their findings to the manager, who by dint of being the only one who was fully dressed was still seen by all the others as being in charge.

"Ah, there you are, Countess," Jim Cross exclaimed, "and... erm... Darren. Good to know you haven't disappeared as well."

He briefly told the two newcomers what had happened, the scream, the bloodstains on the rug—and the missing candlestick, Mister Kumar added hastily—before he announced that 'dear Thea' and Jack Reaper were not present in their rooms.

John Drew turned to Daisy and asked, "May we search your flat, my dear? Maybe the two truants are hiding there?"

"I can assure you that Mrs Slayer and Mr Reaper are *not*

in our flat, sir," Daisy answered icily.

"How can you be so sure, you being blind... and all that? You know what I mean."

There was a sharp intake of breath from Darren at that moment, he seized his wife's hand and squeezed it softly, as if to admonish her not to fly off the handle.

"Mr Drew, you must be joking, right?" Daisy scoffed, "You're not? Well in that case, how about this: you just take my word for it, and if you don't, you call the police, and let *them* check our flat."

"Oh? Ah, erm... sorry, I didn't mean to hurt your feelings. We'll take your word for it, then."

That's when Mister Robbins, who was supposed to be in charge anyway, finally piped up. "Call the police! That's a capital idea! That's exactly what I'm going to do now."

All the guests cried out at once. "Robbins, no, there's no *need* for that! — This is all *staged*, can't you see? — It's part of the *program*, for crying out loud! — We're supposed to *solve* the mystery!"

"That's all very well, but I heard a *horrible* scream, and there's *blood* on the floor, so there."

"Well someone put on an *act*," Anthony Saccharine remarked, "and not convincingly at that. If an attacker hits you over the head with a heavy candlestick, how can you scream like that, I ask you?"

"I don't know," the manager persisted stubbornly, "but I'm the only one who sleeps on the ground floor, so I heard it a lot better than any of you, and it sounded real enough to me. Besides, a very expensive rug has been *ruined!* So I have no choice. I'm calling the police."

"Well, it's your call," Ruth Vine said placatingly, "but you're going to make a fool of yourself."

This was not successful as far as placating went, and Mister Robbins stomped off to his quarters on the side of the hall where his office and his private quarters were situated, slamming the door behind him. The others sighed, and shrugged.

"*Biiig* trouble ahead," Mrs Vine muttered, and Daisy said to no one in particular, "That man is *so* impressionable. Such a bundle of nerves. Always as jumpy as a cat!"

The opportunity to get back at Robbins with a few cheap digs was too good to pass.

— 5 —

When you called the police in the middle of the night to report a murder, you didn't necessarily expect immediate action, but sometimes that was precisely what you got. To start with, the local station would redirect you to the West Sussex CID in Horsham as fast as they could, knowing they had an all-night emergency post on call there, and all too anxious not to get involved in anything they could easily pass on to others.

In theory the CID emergency team consisted of two officers, one with a higher rank than the other, for instance a Detective Sergeant and a Detective Constable. The local CID's 'Governor', Detective Chief Inspector Gilford, had arranged things so that every member of the service did a night shift once or twice a week, with the exception of himself, naturally. These shifts were not popular, but the more practical members of the detective corps used them to catch up on their paperwork. The chances that you would actually have to go out and solve a crime were practically non-existent.

In reality, however, things could turn out slightly differently. Especially if like Constable Hardy you were teamed up with Sergeant Mundie. Hardy did spend the night catching up on his paperwork, sitting right next to the emergency phone, but his 'sarge' always made use of the opportunity to spend the night at The Fly and Fish, having a few beers with his habitual drinking buddies while he was supposed to be on duty. Since the opening hours had been liberalised, the place had become the rowdiest haunt for all-night revellers far and wide, with 'darts and dancing' permanently on the program as a cover to stay open far into the small hours. The pub's original purpose of catering to fly fishers had some-what receded into the background. Before setting off Mundie would tell Hardy, "Come and pick me up if anything unex-pected happens. You know where to find me."

So when Mister Robbins phoned the police in the night of 'the scream', he got DC Hardy on the line, who was all ears, helpful and reassuring, and who promised to send over an 'intervention team' at once. This was more than the caller had hoped for, but as it happened the Constable couldn't believe his luck, although he didn't expect for one moment that anyone had actually been murdered at the Manor Hotel. It seemed rather improbable, but who was he to cast doubts on the claim? It looked like an ideal opportunity to go out and pester the sarge.

Moments later, when he entered the smoky, noisy prem-ises of The Fly and Fish, he had no trouble at all to locate his superior. Sitting in the usual corner, surrounded by the usual gang of rowdy drinking buddies, Sergeant Mundie looked like the biggest and fattest toad in the pool as he raised his pint of Guiness towards the low, dark ceiling.

"Here's to my poor wife, all alone in our empty bed, wor-rying about her darling Trevor who's chasing criminals through the night."

"Hear-hear!" the others cried, raising their pints too, "to the wifeys!"

"What makes you think she's all alone, though, Mundie?" the predictable wit cried, "maybe she's got someone to com-fort her?" And the whole group burst out in manly laughter:

"Bwa-ha-ha!"

"Oh-no-no, not my Lyudmila. She *adores* me. She's the best post-order bride that ever came through the mail."

"Yes, but can't you see? she's having an affair with the postman!"

"Bwa-ha-ha!" again.

Time to spoil the fun, Hardy decided.

So he stepped up to the rowdy group and told his superior about the call he'd just had, and that they needed to drive over to the Manor Hotel in Bottomleigh immediately, for an 'intervention' on a murder case.

"What are you talking about?" Mundie demanded, "this is a joke, right?"

"No Sir, it was the hotel manager himself, a Mister Robbins, who reported it."

"Don't tell me you actually *logged* that call?"

"Of course I did, Sarge, it's the protocol, isn't it?"

That's when Mundie knew he was defeated, and he meekly followed his colleague to the police car parked at the kerb in front of the pub. The two of them drove off in stony silence, but after a while, when Hardy offered him a stick of mint gum, "To cover up the beer on your breath, Sir," his superior mumbled, "Good thinking, mate," as graciously as he could, and added, "Not a word to anyone about where you picked me up, all right?"

"Of course not, Sarge."

When they turned into the manor's park and drove up to the house, Mundie told Hardy to switch on the police car's siren and flashing lights. "Let's wake everybody up in there." The constable obeyed without protesting; it seemed only fair if you were called out for an intervention in the middle of the night. When they entered the huge lobby the entire population of the hotel was coming down the monumental staircase to meet them. Mundie thought that they were displaying a gratifying sense of urgency and an appropriate air of apprehension. With the exception, that is, of a familiar pair, a blind elderly lady and her wheelchair-bound husband, coming out of some big room on the other side of the hall as if they didn't have a worry in the world, as if sauntering through the house in the middle of the night were a perfectly normal activity.

"Mrs Hayes, Mr Miller, let me guess: that room you're just leaving is the crime scene, right?"

"Good evening, Detective Sergeant. You're right, the library is where you want to have a look, although there's no corpse, only some blood on the rug, apparently."

"I hope you didn't touch anything!"

"Of course not. I was only asking Darren to describe the scene to me. You know that in a situation like this I need his eyes."

"Why am I not surprised to find you right on the spot as soon as a murder has been reported?"

Daisy giggled in a girlish way, "You know me, Mundie, I could never resist a crime scene... and I happen to *live* here, as you may recall."

"Very well, in that case you might as well show us around and fill us in on the case."

But before he followed Daisy and Darren into the library, with Hardy in tow, the detective admonished the group of people still assembled in the hall: "Stay right where you are, all of you. Nobody move a muscle, you hear me? I'll be with you in a minute."

Like a perfect host Darren led the two police officers to the bloodstained rug in the middle of the room, and pointed out the missing candlestick on the mantelpiece, while Daisy told them about 'the scream', which she and her husband hadn't heard, but everyone else in the building had. She also reported that two people were missing: "More about that later." Then she explained the background circumstances of the whole affair, that there was a 'Murder Convention' in progress at the hotel, that all the guests were best-selling mystery writers and there was definitely a possibility that this whole thing had been staged.

"What!?" DS Mundie cried, "are you *serious?* So this Mister Robbins of yours lets us come all the way here to investigate a *prank?* I'm going to give that man a piece of my mind!"

"But that's the thing, don't you see? You can't be *sure* it's a prank, can you? Now that you've been involved, you can't get out of it that easily."

"We'll see about that! Where is he? I want to talk to him."

"He's probably where you left him, sir, in the middle of the entrance hall."

The discussion that followed was rather chaotic. Mundie started berating the hotel's manager at once for disturbing the police for nothing, but he made the mistake of doing so in front of the people still waiting in the lobby, who immediately started putting in their oar, all eight of them, one by one.

"Now look here, Officer," Jim Cross started, "I could have told you so all along. This whole thing is a little game of ours, a diverting little puzzle we're supposed to solve."

"It doesn't make any sense anyway," someone else added, "we all came down here within a *minute* of that scream, so how could so much blood have been shed in so little time?"

"And besides, who would produce such a long-drawn scream *after* being hit by a candlestick?"

And so on.

Then, just as Mundie was thinking that he'd better drop the whole affair, Robbins spoiled everything by coming back at him about the rug.

"It's a beautiful and rare piece, you know. Who's going to pay for it?"

"So you called in the CID because of your *rug?*"

"No, no, Inspector, I called the local station, and told them about the *scream*, and the blood on the rug, yes... and *they* redirected me to the CID."

"Same difference, and I'm a detective sergeant, by the way. Still, I have a mind to *close down* this whole place just to show you what's what."

And while the hotel manager started whining about his precious 'establishment', and that the police should avoid 'disturbing' the smooth running of it as much as possible, Mundie realized in a flash that simply pretending that a real crime had taken place would be the best solution. It would solve a number of problems for him, and allow him to get even with this irritating Mister Robbins... and with DC Hardy. Even inspector Gilford, his governor, and probably Mrs Hayes too would be gratifyingly annoyed. Without another word to the obtrusive group of people congregated in front of him, he turned towards his underling and started barking orders.

"Hardy! go to the car at once and call in the forensic intervention team from Division on the radio... yes, I know it's the middle of the night, but they have an emergency post of their own, don't they?"

While the constable trotted off to the car, Mundie turned back towards Mister Robbins and announced that he wanted to take down the depositions of each and every person present on the crime scene. "Can you arrange for a desk in a quiet room, where Hardy and I can have some privacy for the interviews? I'm not asking, actually, so just say yes."

The manager stammered that he and his helper could use his own office, "right here on the ground floor."

"Sounds good. In a moment the forensic people will be swarming all over this place, taking pictures, finger prints, and the whole shebang, so I want everybody out of here and back in their rooms. Robbins, you'll be responsible for bringing in your guests for interrogation one by one, do I make myself clear?"

The guests were quite bewildered, but started trundling up the stairs reluctantly, and Hardy came in and announced that the forensic team was on its way.

"Good. Now *you're* going to take down all those depositions, and I'll want them typed out in full before the end of your shift tonight, got that?"

Finally Mundie turned to Daisy and Darren, who were still lingering in the hall, and asked, "What are you waiting for, Madam? Go back to your flat until you're called."

"Just a word, if I may, Detective Sergeant... Two things... First, you do realize that there's a real chance this whole affair is a hoax? The fact that *two* people are missing is interesting in that respect. It's as if Mrs Slayer and Mr Reaper are telling their colleagues, 'Find out which one of us is the victim, and which is the murderer.' And as long as you don't have a corpse, you don't have much to go on anyway."

"We'll see about that. If forensics find *real* blood on that rug, then we're in business after all. Just leave it to the police, will you?"

"Still, I suggest that you keep this thing under wraps as much as you can. If the press get hold of it they'll go wild, and how will it make you look if it turns out to be a prank? No, believe me, Detective Sergeant, when you interrogate them, better make sure all those best-selling authors keep quiet about it as well. They're all gagging for publicity, you know."

"All right. Fair point. Anything else?"

"Yes. The second thing I wanted to discuss is this. Before you arrived I talked to Mister Kumar, the night porter, and he confided that he was *dozing* behind the reception desk until he was woken by the scream. He'll tell you all that himself, but could you please make sure that Robbins doesn't hear about it? Poor Kumar is awfully afraid to lose his job because of this, you see."

"And why should I care if he does? If the man sleeps on the job, let him face the consequences, I'd say."

At that moment constable Hardy, who'd been standing right next to his superior all the while, cleared his throat and piped up: "Erm... Sarge, may I remind you about what you said to me in the car on our way over?"

"Huh? What are you talking about?"

"You know... not to tell anyone *where* I picked you up to-night?"

"Oh! That! Yes... all right, all right."

II   Many questions don't mean more answers

— 1 —

"What do you think is going to happen now?" Sondra asked, "the guests still seem to think it's some kind of joke, but I don't like those police ribbons across the library door one bit."

"You've just summed up the situation quite nicely," Daisy replied as the receptionist tapped with her hand on a large brown envelope she'd laid in front of her on the desk. Then she said, "Is this for me?"

"Yes, your copy, I've just finished printing the first issue of the 'Daily Bulletin', and like I just told you, the guests don't seem worried at all, as you'll find out when Darren reads it to you."

"Well thanks, Sondra, that's awfully sweet! How's your backache?"

"Getting better, but I wouldn't mind some extra sessions, if that's all right."

"Of course! Come up at the end of your shift if you want, then we can discuss the situation while I work on you."

Daisy handed the envelope to Darren, and they moved over to the lift, she walking behind his chair and pushing lightly while he steered the course. In passing he described the plastic ribbons that cordoned off the library, with white and blue stripes, and the message, "Police line, do not cross," repeated over and over. "Sondra's right, it looks pretty grim."

Back in the flat, Darren opened the envelope and started reading the leaflet it contained out loud for his wife's benefit.

First instalment of the Daily Bulletin
of the Top Ten Club's Murder Convention

Dear friends, as we spent our first day at the Manor Hotel settling in and answering Thea's delightful questionnaire, this here is now our first Daily Bulletin. Little did we know what was awaiting us, yesterday at this time, when we published our answers for everyone's perusal.

Meanwhile we've all experienced an enervating night and participated in a particularly successful start of the Convention's 'entertainment'. Well done, Thea and Jack!

However, it's a pity that the police should have been called in and invaded the place just as the fun was about to begin. They've rather spoiled the game. We must assume that all kinds of interesting clues had been left on the crime scene for us to investigate, but now it is out of bounds, and the clues have probably been destroyed or removed by the forensics people anyway. Unfortunate, but never mind. I would suggest that the eight of us still in the game should set to work regardless, using their imagination rather than basing their contributions on material clues.

We do know that a candlestick has disappeared, but feel free to consider this as a red herring. The real challenge is to decide who's the victim and who the killer. I would also suggest that the two miscreants who caused all the drama last night may come out of hiding, now that their little charade has been so lustily sabotaged by the local cops.

We're hoping to hear more tomorrow, from the pen of another participant, and to be able to publish your first contributions about the mystery at hand.

Yours, for this brief Bulletin, **Q Anon**

"That must be Lee Quincy," Daisy said, "and the first question that comes to mind is: was the clue *we* found on the crime scene planted there as part of an elaborate game, or is it real?"

"You tell me, precious," Darren answered.

"Well, it could go both ways, you know. That's the annoying thing about this little snippet of singed paper: it doesn't tell us much."

That night, when Mister Robbins had stomped off to call the police, and the guests had sauntered back up the stairs to their rooms, discussing the events animatedly among themselves, only Daisy and Darren had remained in the hall with Mister Kumar. Daisy had started sounding him out at once, as she and Darren had missed the whole thing and she was eager to know what had happened. That's when the night porter had confessed that he'd been fast asleep, and begged her not to tell his boss, whispering urgently, casting nervous glances towards the closed door of the manager's office. Daisy had reassured him, and as Robbins had not reappeared, she'd asked if she and her husband could take a look at the crime scene. "But of course, Madam, you *live* here," their new friend had replied, still whispering, and so they'd silently slipped into the library.

"Make sure we don't leave any traces, darling."

"Sure thing, precious, just stay behind me."

Darren steered them to the middle of the room to take a better look at the blood-stained carpet, but first he described the whole setup to his wife. The vast floor held several reading tables with easy chairs around them, and different coffee tables with sets of sofas and comfortable armchairs. "But you know all that, don't you, precious? This place hasn't changed that much since the old days."

In the middle of the room there were no tables, no lounge sets, the floor was free, and covered with a large Persian rug. This was where the blood stains were conspicuously visible, and Darren took a closer look at them.

"They seem real enough, as far as I can tell, but if someone was hit over the head with a candlestick, the killer must have run quite a distance from the chimney over there to the middle of the room, where we are now."

"All right; interesting. If the victim was just leaving the room it's not unthinkable that he or she was attacked from behind."

"It's also not unthinkable that the body was carried away through the French windows, and you know why? One of those are still wide open, *but the curtains are drawn to hide the fact.*"

"Also interesting. So the dead body could have been pushed right through the curtains, right?"

"Yep... but do you think a murder actually happened here?"

"I'm just testing the *possibilities*, that's all... For one thing, if the two people involved were standing by the mantelpiece to start with, what were they doing there? Was there a *fire* in the grate?"

"Let's have a look."

They moved over to the fireplace, Darren peering inside intently, Daisy sniffing at the air like a bloodhound.

"I can smell burnt wood all right, but there's no telling if the hearth doesn't always smell like that."

"And I can see that some papers have been burned to a crisp recently, but there's no telling when."

"I'd like to feel if the hearth is still warm. Do you think I can?"

"Sure, just step around and kneel down in front of me. It doesn't look like there's anything still burning in there, or whatever."

So Daisy knelt in front of the fireplace and prodded the ashes and charred wood chunks cautiously while Darren looked on. Then she pressed her hand down on the stone bottom under the ashes, and pulled it back immediately. "Ouch! it's still quite hot. There's definitely been a fire recently."

"And there's a little piece of paper lying next to the ashes, almost against the side wall on your left."

Daisy prodded the floor of the hearth, Darren guiding her hand verbally, "Just a bit more to the back... there it is," and soon she picked up a tiny fragment of charred paper and handed it over to him. He described an irregular lozenge with singed edges, and words from a typewriter still clearly visible. He read the words out loud:

```
ather
    shrewd prey
  ing in the doorway
  tell me why you're getting so
don't even know myself. But while we're
      would take too long to expl
          occurred to him
              disap
```

"How extraordinary!" Daisy exclaimed, "it sounds like a piece of dialogue, it must be from the typewritten manuscript of a novel or something."

"Yes, and my guess would be that it was torn to pieces before it was thrown in the fire."

Just at that moment the police had arrived with a howling siren and flashing blue lights, and the two had hurried out of the library. Daisy was dusting off her fingers and Darren was hiding their find between his thighs when the detective sergeant had spotted them, both looking as innocent as anything.

Daisy had spent that day investigating what she called "the fire in the grate". As soon as the chambermaids and cleaning ladies had arrived in the morning, she'd come down and asked around about what the normal routine was regarding the fireplace in the library. But first she'd had to tell all the 'girls' what had happened the night before, and why those police ribbons were there. The day staff had missed all the excitement! Daisy assured them that she and Darren had actually slept through the whole thing as well.

Anyway, it turned out that a fire was lit in the library after dinner every evening, "for the cosy atmosphere", and that it was left to burn itself out after the staff had left. "There are always some logs in a wicker basket for the guests to keep the fire going if they want, but they rarely put on more logs." The ashes were cleared in the morning, but on that day, as the library was out of bounds, no one had been allowed to enter it.

"Isn't it dangerous to leave a fire unattended like this?" Daisy asked Agnieszka, "with the wooden floor and all those rugs, there's something of a fire hazard, no?"

"Not to mention a *looot* of books! But it's okay, really, the fireplace is safe, there's a bit of stone floor around it, and the night porter is supposed to keep an eye on it, that's part of his job."

Except when he's sound asleep, Daisy reflected.

"And does it happen often that people burn *papers* in the

chimney?"

"No, never."

"And how about *relighting* the fire in the middle of the night? And I mean around half past one, so: really late."

"That shouldn't be a problem for anyone who knows anything about fires. The logs are already there, and some paper to use as kindle is easy to find. But I can't tell you how many logs are missing now…"

"I know, the hearth is out of bounds."

So now the question remained: was the fragment of paper they'd found all that was left of a burned manuscript, or had it been planted in sight of the bloodstained rug as part of an elaborate game? There was no telling.

And should they inform the police about their find? The forensics team had showed up *after* they'd removed the snippet from the crime scene; they only took it away because they weren't *expecting* the library to be taken over by them and cordoned off, as Daisy pointed out to Darren.

"Should I call my old friend DCI Gilford and come clean about it?"

"No need, precious, he will come to see you soon enough. The guy can't resist your charms and shows up pronto as soon as gets the chance."

"Oh, go away!"

"Even Mundie seemed glad enough to see you again last night."

When Sondra came in for her session, Daisy showed her the snippet as well. The receptionist had heard about "the find" too, and was curious about it, and as she'd given her a copy of the 'bulletin', Daisy couldn't refuse her the pleasure in her turn of having a look at the intriguing fragment of typewritten text. At least she knew what to talk about while she started working on her patient's stiff lower vertebrae in her guest room.

"The thing is, this is exactly what 'Q Anon' had in mind when he mentioned 'interesting clues' that were supposed to have been left on the scene, but actually lighting a fire to make it look real... I don't know."

"Who's this 'Q Anon' anyway?" Sondra mumbled, her voice muffled because she was resting her forehead on her folded arms.

"Probably Lee Quincy, as 'Anon' simply stands for 'anonymous', you know what I mean?"

"Oh, yeah... but you don't think it's all part of a game?"

"No, I'm finding that hard to believe. For starters, who would ruin an expensive rug just to set up a puzzle? Theodora Slayer seems a perfectly decent kind of lady to me, even quite old-fashioned. She would never do a thing like that... So I don't agree with the 'Daily Bulletin' at all, but maybe those people have been *led* to expect this kind thing? They know Thea better than we do."

"Yes, but why do you have such a problem with the fire? At least that part of the stunt didn't cause any damage to the hotel's property."

"No, but there it's my imagination running away with me... You see, if one of these writers had stolen the manuscript of Thea's latest novel, say, and if she'd caught him in the act of burning it, wouldn't that be a motive for murder? If this is the only copy she had, imagine her rage when she saw it burning bright in the chimney... it would be enough to bash the perpetrator's head with a candlestick while he walked away from his misdeed!"

Silently Daisy decided she would have to interrogate Mister Kumar again when he came in, ask him if 'the scream' could have been a cry of rage instead of howl of terror or pain.

Meanwhile Sondra sniggered, "This is exactly the kind of story the members of the club would like to see in the next bulletin! If you want, I can include your contribution tomorrow, without naming you, but then perhaps you would also have to explain *why* the guy would have destroyed a colleague's work?"

"Yeah, that I don't know, and Thea is even less likely to bash in someone's head than to ruin a rug, so there's that too."

"But what do you think is going to *happen* next?"

"Well, obviously we're waiting for the police to make their next move. My old friend Mundie, although he's an obnoxious little prat in general, made an interesting observation last night. He said that all will depend on what forensics will find out about the blood on that rug. I suppose they rolled it up and took the whole thing away to their lab. If they find real blood, as opposed to ketchup or blood from a pig, say, then this charming little club is going to get a lot more on their plates than they bargained for."

"I never thought I would ever say this," Sondra sighed, "but I can't wait to hear from the police."

— 2 —

DCI Gilford also sighed deeply while he poured over the reports of the so-called murder case. What on earth had gotten into DS Mundie this time? First the Manor Hotel's manager, that hysterical fool, calls in the middle of the night to report an alleged murder, and that idiot of a sergeant, who normally would avoid work like the plague, goes and acts on it immediately… how was this even possible? Then it turns out that there's no corpse, and that the hotel is hosting this crazy 'Murder Convention', yet Mundie unleashes the whole rigmarole of 'securing the crime scene' and calls in the poor chaps from forensics, also in the middle of the night. Now there was a big stack of papers lying on Gilford's desk: Mundie's reports, lab results, and the witness statements of a dozen people, including those of a bunch of *mystery writers!*

Gilford sighed, and looked over through the glass partition of his cubicle at the culprit, sitting innocently at his desk in the main room of the department, pretending to be working hard on the case, like the colleagues around him in the vast open office space. They were checking the backgrounds of all the hotel guests, using computers, mainly. Gilford sighed, because he was in no position to complain. That he had to go through a whole stack of papers was entirely due to the fact that he had no idea how a computer worked, and no intention to learn, thank you very much. At his age, and with his rank, no one could expect or demand it of him. His underlings had to 'print out' the paperwork and present it to him in nice, old-fashioned cardboard folders, but the problem with this approach was that these computers made it possible to produce an endless stream of documents, apparently, a great deal more than any police officer would ever have managed to do on a typewriter.

Also, Gilford couldn't challenge Mundie about his unexpected—and untypical—bout of zeal, for the simple reason that the results of the forensic lab had come back, and it turned out that the bloodstains on the rug were *human blood* all right, type AB negative, a pretty rare one. Mundie was on the phone at that moment, trying to find out if there was a match with one of the two allegedly missing people. The sergeant looked up, sensing that he was being observed perhaps, and saw his boss watching him, so he waved at Gilford. Sarcastically, Gilford thought. The bastard!

It was uncanny. Take the laziest and most incompetent detective, Mundie, incapable of following any rules or sticking to procedure, who will never resist a shortcut where he can find one, gratingly obnoxious and opinionated at all times, and that is precisely the detective who turns out to have a *nose* for ferreting out crimes, an animal instinct, an infallible gut feeling. There was no other explanation possible for what had happened the night before last. It even accounted for the uncharacteristic bout of zeal. And the galling thing was that Gilford himself lacked this talent completely. He'd never perceived the least bit of sleuthing instinct in himself, he had to admit it. That was precisely why he was such a drudge, and a stickler for rules and procedures. That, in its turn, was why he was in charge here. Time to show them who's boss, he decided. He stepped out of his glass cubicle and walked over to the crime chart in the main room, the shiny whiteboard where the photos of all the participants of the Murder Convention were pinned up with tiny magnets, along with those of the manager, the night porter, and their old acquaintances, Mrs Hayes and Mr Miller.

"All right now, listen up, chaps," Gilford snapped, and it was all he could do not to clap in his hands like an overbearing headmaster. "I want you people to wrap up the background checks now. The moment has come to concentrate on the *timeline* of what the devil happened in that manor's library in the middle of the night. We have to reconstitute every movement of every person involved, minute by minute, hour by hour, including those that have gone missing. And not only during that fateful night, as most people claim to have been asleep in their own room anyway. No. I want you to create a clear overview of what happened on the day before, who spoke to whom, when exactly the two possible victims were last seen by the others. Check if all the stories tally, bring to light any discrepancies or inconsistencies, verify each alibi inasmuch as it is feasible... Have you got all that? Then let's get on with it, chop-chop!"

Mundie started groaning in a rather gratifying way.

"Yes, Sergeant, now that we know that we're dealing with

human blood, we have no choice but to pursue this matter relentlessly... *Relentlessly*, do you hear me?"

That would show them.

Meanwhile, at the Manor Hotel, the second edition of the Daily Bulletin had been printed, and Darren read the copy Sondra had given them to his wife. The eight participants still in the running had dutifully submitted their contributions, as the first redactor had proposed. These were just brief scenarios of what could have happened in 'the night of the scream', all of them rather sketchy and tongue-in-cheek, suggesting that the contributors weren't putting all their heart into it.

"I can understand that," Daisy muttered when Darren had read a few texts, "this whole setup was rather bleak to start with, and now that Thea and Jack are still missing, it's becoming a bit too disturbing to be fun."

And that was exactly what Ruth Vine, the redactor of the second Bulletin also expressed in her leader: "When are the two 'actors' who set up the game finally going to come out of hiding? Enough is enough, already!" she concluded in her piece.

But the contributions were interesting all the same. Every option seemed to have been covered. Jack had killed Thea, then made the body disappear, before fleeing himself to evade the police. Or Thea had killed Jack. Or someone had killed Thea and Jack both, "In which case the killer is still among us." Or perhaps Jack and Thea were lovers and had decided to elope, rather than go through with this tedious Convention where they couldn't get any opportunity to be alone. The clues, mostly invented by the contributors themselves, were interesting as well, inasmuch as they revealed that nobody had noticed the charred papers in the fireplace, nor had anyone thought of interrogating Mister Kumar, so the fact that he'd been asleep hadn't come to light either. "We're still two clues ahead of the crowd," Daisy noted.

"A fat lot of difference that makes," Darren sniggered.

Nevertheless, Daisy had managed to talk to the night porter, and this little interview had yielded some interesting information. Mister Kumar couldn't for the life of him tell if 'the scream' had been in anguish or in anger, but what he could ascertain without any doubt whatsoever, was that it had been 'produced' by a woman. "A beautiful soprano, in fact, Madam," he'd elaborated politely, "I'm something of an opera buff myself, you see, and even in our traditional music back home we have ladies who master that kind of voice to perfection." At least that was something. Kumar had also confirmed that the guests on the first floor had called down to him within half a minute after the scream had roused him. "In fact it was Mister Adam who asked me what was going on."

Another intriguing piece of information the night porter had imparted, was that he'd been dreaming of Mrs Slayer just before he woke up. "It was a confusing experience for me, Mrs Hayes, first because I hardly know the lady, and secondly I was only half asleep, you understand, so when the scream jogged me wide awake, I could distinctly remember that she'd just been crying 'I changed the names! I changed the names!' in my dream."

Could this have been something the dear man had overheard, coming from the library, *before* he woke up, in fact? An interesting clue, at any rate, that no one else seemed to have registered.

On the other hand, several of the mystery writers had had the brilliant idea to check the parking lot, and discovered that only Jack Reaper's Jaguar was missing, and not Thea's Bentley, "Which is neither here nor there," someone wrote, "for if Thea had killed Jack, she could easily have pocketed his car keys as well."

"Funny how these people seem to know *exactly* which car belongs to whom," Daisy remarked.

"That's quite normal, sweetness, your problem is that you're not one bit car-minded."

"I guess that's my excuse for not thinking of checking this myself."

But still, it was important to know that one car had gone missing.

— 3 —

When the police turned up the next morning, DCI Gilford was with them. Three sturdy vehicles scrunched on the front-drive gravel in rapid succession, and two or three men emerged from each one and stormed into the hotel. Although there were not even ten of them all told, it felt as if a swarm of locusts had descended on a peaceful and defenceless land. The idea was to marshal as much of the CID's resources as could be dispensed with in order to carry out the task at hand in as short a timescale as possible; you couldn't mobilize too many people for too long on such a doubtful case.

First the men conducted a thorough search of the hotel's premises under the supervision of their Chief, and with the reluctant assistance of the manager, but to no avail. They soon had to draw the conclusion that neither a corpse, nor a pair of playful schemers could be hidden anywhere on the premises. So Gilford gave orders to interrogate the guests, and while his men started working on the hapless participants of the Convention, he himself went straight up to the attic and was graciously invited in by Daisy and Darren. The hostess was just about to pour some tea, and her husband fetched an extra cup for him from under the kitchen counter and brought it over to the sitting area in his wheelchair, an action to be greatly admired indeed. DCI Gilford explained what was happening downstairs, and assured his hosts that he did not consider them as suspects in any way. "I understand you didn't even hear the scream, and came down much later than the others that night."

"That's right, Inspector, but I'm a bit surprised that you and your men have come out in force like this... You do realize that there's still a strong possibility that this whole thing might only be a hoax?"

"Yes, yes, I appreciate that, Madam, and that's the first thing I'd like to ask you: do you reckon it *is?*"

"Ah, that's the difficulty, right there. All the guests seem to think so, but I've had my doubts from the start. Mrs Slayer is not one to ruin a valuable rug for a trifle, and she and her accomplice should have shown themselves again by now if it was only a game."

"Quite right. Besides, Mundie's reports have placed the case in a rather dramatic light, and that is all I have to go on."

"I understand. It's the same Mundie, by the way, who said something rather astute to me the other night: that all would depend on what exactly the forensic specialists would find on that rug. Do you have any news about that?"

"I do, but I'm not at liberty to disclose anything."

"How annoying! You've just told us that we're not suspects, so why the secrecy? Anyway, I have two pieces of information for you that are not in Mundie's reports. Darren and I had just been snooping around a little before he arrived, I suppose I might as well confess this right away."

Gilford chuckled comfortably at these words. "I more or less expected that much, or should I say I even counted on it? Out with it, then, let's hear the whole story!"

So Daisy asked Darren to give the inspector the little piece of paper they'd found, and he had to roll over to his low-slung writing desk, where he picked it up. When he came back and handed it over to their guest, he stayed right next to his armchair while Daisy explained that a fire had been lighted that night, before the dramatic events took place, that some papers appeared to have been burned, and that this fragment was all there was left of them. She also told him about the night porter's testimony, that he'd been dozing until 'the scream' had roused him rather brusquely.

"Obviously these elements don't tell us anything about whether we're dealing with a game or a genuine tragedy. On the contrary, they could point in both directions. Still, there's one interesting detail that I'd like to submit to you. This snippet that was spared by the fire comes from a typewriter. I know for a fact that Mrs Slayer is the only one who still writes her books on such an old-fashioned machine, all the others use computers. This was a topic of discussion I overheard during a coffee break in the library... So: what if Thea Slayer caught Jack Reaper red-handed while he was burning her latest novel in the middle of the night? What if it was the only copy she had? Wouldn't that be enough for her to scream with rage and hit him over the head with a candlestick?"

Gilford sniggered again. "What a vivid imagination you have, my dear! But how would the lady have disposed of the body? We're told the witnesses appeared on the scene within minutes."

"Well, what if Thea had only *wounded* Jack, and regretted her action at once? So she took him to the nearest hospital, in *his* car, exiting through the French windows... I have no idea *how much* blood there is on that rug, mind you, but it's a possible scenario, no?"

"Well, yes, not bad, except it's *Mrs Slayer's* blood that was found. Blood of the type AB negative, very rare, and she's the only one who has it."

"Oh, all right, so she *is* the victim… and have you noticed, my dear Inspector, how I've just *winkled* that information out of you?"

"Really! So you made up this whole story only to trick me?"

"Oh no, I'm perfectly serious about the story. And even if it's Thea's blood on the rug, have you checked the local hospitals, in case she was admitted with some open wound?"

"Naturally, and it turns out she was not hospitalized anywhere around here."

"Still, it goes to show that this is a wide-open case. It could be a staged puzzle, or a tragic accident, or it could be a carefully plotted murder attempt by someone who hopes to have devised the perfect crime."

"Really? And how would that work?"

"Just let me think… I was assuming that Thea could have set this up to get rid of her younger rival… but it could also work the other way round. Yes. If Jack is the one who *suggested* this little puzzle, and if he *enlisted* the help of his intended victim, what better way would there be to eliminate her? Just make it look like a staged act, where both the corpse and the murderer disappear, and it's anybody's guess which is which. By the time people cotton on to the fact that there's been foul play, the perpetrator could have flown to Brazil, or anywhere else."

"Interesting," DCI Gilford said. *I could use this in my next report*, he thought, *'Wide open case… from a damnable hoax to the perfect crime.' Yes, sounds good.* He glanced over at the wheelchair-bound husband, who was still parked right next to where he was sitting, a bit too close for comfort, and he smiled uneasily. You had to make allowances for such a man.

"I don't suppose," Daisy went on, "that you've transmitted Jack's picture and particulars to all the police stations in the country yet, or passed on his car's number to the traffic patrols, and asked the authorities at the airports to keep an eye out for him?"

"No, nothing like that, I'm afraid. To tell you the truth, we're facing a strange conundrum here, Mrs Hayes. You and I both agree that something bad *could* have happened, especially now that we know that it's human blood that we found on the rug, and that it belonged to Mrs Slayer. And at first I assumed that this would be sufficient to open an investigation. Only, it turned out differently, I must confess."

He went on to explain that the local coroner, as well as the man from the Crown Prosecution Service, not to mention the Division Commissioner, had all insisted that the police was to treat this whole thing strictly like a missing persons case for the time being. "Without a corpse there's no murder, as far as they're concerned, so I can only investigate a *disappearance*".

"Yet you came out in force."

"Yes, because even for a missing persons case I can still interrogate witnesses, piece together a timeline, check alibis and such. All the normal footwork that I can achieve with my regular team. But alerting the traffic police or the airports, no."

"That's a shame, sir, there are so many things you could be doing right now, like draining the pond on the grounds. If someone has been murdered that's the first place where you'd have to go looking for a dead body, I guess… And how about the dogs? Surely they would be able to follow any scent left by the two missing people and give you an idea about how they left the premises."

"Yes, it's funny that you should mention that: I left constable Hardy behind at the CID to organize a K9 Unit intervention. They will be here shortly. It takes some time. But there's something else in the line of simple police work where you might be able to be of assistance, Mrs Hayes."

"Of course, anything you say, if I can help."

"I need your expertise as someone who knows Bottom-leigh House through and through. Do you know any secret hiding places on the premises? My men and I have been searching the place thoroughly, but we could find nothing. So do you have suggestions about anything we might have overlooked? You know what I mean: invisible nooks and crannies where people could lie low, lock away a prisoner, or keep a dead body wrapped up in plastic... The dogs might help us when they arrive, but it would be useful to know where to bring them in the first place."

"I see, yes. Well, I'm afraid that such hiding places have been completely spoiled by the reconversion of the old place into a fancy hotel. The beautiful modern flat around you is a case in point: this used to be a dark, cluttered attic where children played hide and seek for hours on end... and look at it now. However, I wonder, we used to get in through one of the basement windows... and would that doctored latch still exist? Are you interested in the possibility that someone from outside might have entered the house undetected?"

"But of course! Could you show me?"

"Certainly. Let's go down at once. It was the fourth basement window around the right-hand corner from the front of the house."

— 4 —

Sergeant Mundie knew that this chap Lee Quincy *knew*. They'd spotted one another at The Fly and Fish two nights back, on *that* night. Therefore Quincy had an ironclad alibi, and Mundie a big problem.

"Listen, Quincy," he hissed after pulling him into a quiet

corner of the lobby, "you didn't see me the other night, you hear? And I certainly couldn't have seen you. So I'll write down that you were at The Fly and Fish all right, but don't count on me to vouch for you."

"Well, I find that rather rich! I have an unassailable alibi, and I'm the only person here who has one, and now you're telling me that I can't even rely on the testimony of a frigging *police* officer?"

"Have a heart, Quincy. You know how it'll look with my boss: I was supposed to be on duty that night, I could lose my job if he hears about this... Besides, you were as drunk as a skunk, and you've testified that you drove back to the hotel afterwards, so you could get a big fat fine and lose your licence for drunk driving if any of this comes to light. I'll make sure of it."

"Hah! Listen who's talking. You were drunk too, and I don't buy this: even you can't fine me just like that, after the fact... You should have busted me straightaway, caught me in the act, but you were too tight yourself at the time."

"Technicalities, eh? Don't be so sure, my friend, I can still make a lot of trouble for you."

"Well, would you go to the trouble of committing *perjury* before a court of law? You were there and you saw me, and that's a fact."

"Court of law? What are you talking about? It won't come to that, you fool! There's enough *other* people that saw you. I'll put *them* in my report as witnesses. Your alibi is safe, so just be nice about this, okay?"

Meanwhile, in another corner, John Drew, the legal eagle of the police procedural was getting on the nerves of another detective: "Do you have a search warrant from a judge?" he demanded, "and are you interrogating me under caution? I know my rights!"

Not far from there Aggie Maple was openly flirting with *her* interrogator, attracting envious glances from his colleagues.

In other words, the mighty bloodhounds from the Horsham CID were in the process of rounding up all the suspects of the Murder Convention in the hotel lobby and squeezing them for information, when their Chief emerged from the lift in the company of the blind lady from the attic loft flat with her wheelchair-bound husband. They formed a strange little trio: the familiar, gangly 'headmaster' who was their boss, the dignified elderly lady with her dark round glasses pushing the chair of the much younger 'wheelie Messiah', who seemed to be steering the course for them both. The detectives couldn't help staring at them in precisely the manner their Mommas had always told them *not* to. What were these three up to now? They made straight for the front entrance of the hotel, the Chief motioning his underlings to carry on with whatever they were doing with a wave of his hand, and he left the premises through the hissing, sliding glass door.

The three of them went down the ramp from the monumental portico to the front drive, where Darren had to work the push rings of his wheels with his hands in order to plough through the gravel, leading the small group around the corner to where the cars were parked. On this side of the building there was a terrace wall, with basement windows close to the ground, and Daisy told them to take her to the fourth skylight in the row. When they'd reached it she stooped, groped around a bit, found the latch, and after turning the handle with both hands she gave it a mighty push. The window gave way with a creaking sound.

"There you are," she said, "normally you should only be able to open it from the inside, but Ralph, my first husband, doctored it when he was a kid, before the war. Actually he just mounted it backwards so the handle would be on the outside, but no one ever noticed. And I had a feeling these basement rooms under the terrace hadn't been renovated, so… some things never change in old houses."

She cautiously pushed the window frame wider. "Voila. This one opens all the way, and then you can slip down into the cellar below. Child's play."

"Extraordinary!" Gilford exclaimed, "but would you say it has been used recently? It sounded rather creaky."

"You're right, it probably hasn't been opened for ages, I don't think… but it does show that in a big house like this there are always many ways of getting in or out. Proof of concept, don't you agree?"

Darren muttered, "So many doors, *sooo* many windows."

"I guess you're right, sir. And we're not far from the spot where Jack Reaper's Jaguar was parked, but we've got no smoking gun for now."

As the three of them were pondering the significance or lack thereof of this discovery, several cars could be heard scrunching on the gravel around the corner. "That will be the reinforcements I was waiting for," Gilford announced.

"You mean the K9 Unit, and constable Hardy?"

"Indeed. I will leave you now, if I may."

But that was counting without this strange couple's sticking power. As the Chief sped off with wide strides of his long legs, Darren and Daisy followed closely on his heels, he mightily pumping at the wheel rims of the chair, she pushing from behind as hard as she could, their coordination apparently well-rehearsed by long practice. Even the gravel couldn't keep them back. When they reached the drive again, Darren described what was happening under his breath. A couple of police dogs were being taken out of a kennel van by their handlers, impatiently pulling at their short leashes, and from the back of another van the rolled-up Persian rug was being unloaded. Then the rug, the dogs, and the police officers ascended the stairs of the colonnaded portico in a brisk procession and entered the hotel. They were closely followed by a wheelchair speeding up the ramp, with a hurrying blind lady trotting behind it.

DCI Gilford and his men made straight for the library, their plan of action clear enough: put the Persian rug back in place and the dogs on the scent of the blood stains it contained. But at first they were taken aback by the presence of an interloper sitting on his knees on the spot where they planned to unroll the rug, thoroughly scrutinizing the floor with an old-fashioned magnifying glass.

"Who are you?" the Chief thundered, "What the dickens do you think you're doing here?"

"Oh, ah, Chief Inspector, I'm so sorry. As the police line had been removed I thought it would be okay to have a look around."

"That, sir, is a completely wrong conclusion! What are you looking for? Dropped something or left traces on the crime scene, did you? Your presence here is highly suspect, to put it mildly, and I could have you arrested at once for Tampering with Evidence."

The intruder stammered some more apologies and Daisy, who'd just caught up with the Chief, piped up right next to his shoulder, "It's all right, Inspector. This is the famous Anthony Saccharine and he writes forensic mysteries. He couldn't help himself, poor man."

"Well I never! What a crazy bunch we have here... Would you please leave the premises immediately, sir, and let us get on with our work? Thank you very much."

While the writer hurried off Daisy squeezed Darren's hand. Clearly they weren't included in the Chief's orders and they discreetly stayed put by his side. Meanwhile the rug had been unrolled and the first police dog was led to it by his handler. Daisy could hear the animal sniffing around excitedly, then yelp impatiently, probably pulling on its leash, already on the trail. A scent dog, she knew, would be able to plainly perceive each step that had been taken by any person in the process of carrying a body or leading a wounded victim out of the room. A second dog likewise 'gave voice' to indicate that it had picked up the spoor. Both handlers, pulled by their dogs, made a beeline for one of the French windows, the one that had been left open on 'the night of the scream'. The chief inspector, Hardy, and the two helpers who'd 'organized' the rug followed closely. Finally Darren made sure that he and his darling wife tagged along as well.

The procession came out onto the terrace at the back of the house, walked around the empty swimming pool, then veered onto the lawn that surrounded it, which Mister Robbins would have frowned upon, but they were following the dogs. (Where had their charming hotel manager gone to anyway, Daisy wondered. Probably being submitted to the third degree in his own office!) A shallow slope of the lawn led them down from the terrace to the parking lot by the side of the house, and both dogs, one after the other, came to a sudden halt on the exact spot where Jack Reaper's Jaguar had been standing until 'the night of the scream'.

The chief inspector looked around him, as if to say "How about that?" to his underlings, and muttered, more to himself than to them, "So they drove off from here, eh? We must make sure to ask the witnesses if they heard the sound of a car that night."

Darren, who'd parked himself right by his side couldn't help himself, and piped up: "It could have left silently, Chief. Bottomleigh House stands at the top of an almost invisible slope. But in a Jag it's still easy enough to let yourself roll down to the gate by the main road in complete silence. Then you can drive off to anywhere in England."

Gilford jumped, just a little. "Are you still there, Mr Miller? And you too, Mrs Hayes? We're back at the spot where we started, what?"

"That's right, sir, almost at the foot of the terrace wall again... and didn't I mention the French windows before as a possible escape route?"

"Yes, I believe you did."

But their exchange was interrupted by one of the scent dogs giving voice again, and pulling his handler from the parking spot straight to the wall, where it stopped in front of one of the low windows, and started barking excitedly. This was not the same basement skylight Daisy had shown to the inspector, but one situated several positions down the row. The glass pane closest to the latch had been neatly broken, creating a round hole through which one could reach the handle inside.

"There you are, Sir" the dog handler told the Chief, "obviously a place of unlawful entry."

"How extraordinary!" Gilford exclaimed, "are you telling me that the corpse *could have been carried inside again* through this window? We searched those basements earlier this morning and we didn't find anything there."

"No, no, there's no stiff in there, Sir, that's not what my K9 is telling us. For the hounds, the corpse, or a bleeding person, is only the *starting point* of the trail. They also follow the scent of any person involved in *displacing* the victim. What I think must have happened, is that someone *from outside* helped carry the body to the car, and that same person has been brought here *beforehand*, in the same car. So the dog picked up this person's scent in the parking lot, but it has no way of knowing *when* the trail was created."

"How extraordinary!" Gilford repeated, "I thought Reaper killed Mrs Slayer on the spur of the moment and dragged her body to his car through a French window, so why on earth would he have brought someone to the hotel beforehand? What do *you* make of it, my dear Mrs Hayes?"

"Isn't the answer obvious? If an *accomplice* was enlisted

from the start, the killing wasn't 'on the spur of the moment' after all. No dragging of the corpse either, that would have left traces on the floor and in the grass, no? Believe me, as a physiotherapist I know all too well how heavy and unwieldy the body of an unresponsive adult can be. So if Jack Reaper, say, *intended* to kill Thea Slayer, he might have enlisted someone *in advance* to help him carry the body away."

— 5 —

"They're not going to solve the case by waiting for a corpse to turn up spontaneously," Daisy told Darren that afternoon after the police had left.

"Well, maybe they *will* solve it by waiting patiently for the two ringleaders who set up this hoax to turn up?"

"You still believe that's a possibility? It was *Thea's blood* on that rug, you know."

"I know, I'm only trying to cheer you up."

"You're right, in a way. Even Thea's blood could be part of a hoax, if they really wanted to put it on."

Daisy was rather miffed by the way Gilford had suddenly wrapped up the investigation, just before it was time for lunch. After the scent dogs had been taken away in their kennel van by their handlers, he'd asked his detectives to wind down their interviews and to gather all the remaining participants of the Murder Convention in the entrance hall of the Manor Hotel. Sondra and Robbins were also present, as well as the couple of 'permanent residents' from the attic flat. Everybody had been dying to hear what the Chief had to say. But he only told the assembled authors that this would be all for now, that he was going to write up his report, and that he wanted them to carry on with their convention as planned.

66

"I can't force anyone, but I would be grateful if you all stayed here for another week or so, until the end of the period that has already been booked, say. By that time we'll know more, and we'll get back to you if we need any extra information. Thank you."

"So that's it?" Daisy had mumbled, ostensibly under her breath, but loud enough for everyone to hear, "there's not going to be any further investigation?"

"No, Madam, I'm afraid not. We have enough on our plate already, you know, more important fish to fry, many irons in the fire and all that."

"*What*? another crime wave in West Sussex?"

"Don't push it, Mrs Hayes."

And then the swarm of locusts had flown away as fast and as unexpectedly as it had descended on them earlier on, apparently bent on devouring their lunch elsewhere. Meanwhile Daisy and Darren had polished off a lunch of their own in their flat, and now they were having their usual post-prandial little stroll on the manor's grounds, walking on a circuit around the pond in the park.

"What I should have told Gilford," Daisy reflected, "is that if only he would *assume* that a murder has taken place, and investigate accordingly, the killer would eventually be able to tell the police what happened to the body, when he or she was arrested... You always come up too late with what you should have said."

"Well why don't you go and find the killer yourself then?" Darren said as cheerfully as he could, "it's what you always do, isn't it?"

"Normally, yes, but I have to admit that I'm a bit stumped in this case. For one thing, I wish we could get someone to empty this pond for us, but Robbins would never allow it."

"No, and you can't blame him. Besides, the dogs definitely didn't think the corpse had been carried to the pond."

"True. There's that."

"What I'm looking forward to is the third Daily Bulletin, see what the members of the club make of it all."

"Well, I'm less and less interested in what these fine ladies and gentlemen have to say. Let's not forget that they're all suspects as well, they had enough means and opportunities, not to mention loads of motives, so some of them could definitely be involved, somehow... It makes my flesh crawl just to think about it."

"In that case, that's a possible line of investigation right there, although the 'suspects' will probably tell you that it's none of your business."

"True again. Like I said, I'm a bit stumped."

"Still, what do you want to do about it? It seems to me there's precious little you can do. You'll just have to leave it alone for the time being, or am I only wasting my breath when I'm saying so?"

"Yes, you are," his wife replied behind him with a rueful smile in her voice, before she gave his wheelchair a mighty shove.

When they re-entered the lobby, Sondra was ticking away on her computer behind the reception desk. She interrupted her breakneck typing to greet them with her usual joviality. "I'm just 'inputting' today's Bulletin," she explained, "the authors are still keeping me busy; good thing I have little else to do right now. I'll send up your copy as soon as I've printed it, yes?"

"Sure," Daisy replied, "although I'm losing interest somewhat, but Darren is still looking forward to it."

"What's this?" Sondra tutted, "feeling a bit put off, are we? A bit frustrated? I'm starting to see why the police chief likes you so much, you have more drive than any of his men. But he could've shown a bit more appreciation, like by putting *you* in charge of the case if he no longer wants it."

"Don't put ideas in her head," Darren grumbled, "I'm having enough trouble with her as it is… But what's the general mood with the writers?"

"The consensus right now is that something awful did actually happen, and everyone is trying to figure out what it could be… They're all stating the obvious and repeating themselves a bit."

"Same here with Daisy. But it sounds interesting still."

His wife gave the wheelchair another hard shove, and pushed Darren towards the elevator in a huff. "See you later, Sondra!" he cried.

Back at the flat Daisy asked, "Is there anything interesting on the telly, darling?"

"I'm afraid not, precious."

"Or shall we listen to the radio?"

"If that can put your mind off your troubles… but I've just been thinking, you know, during the ride up: weren't you all fired up by the little piece of paper we found in the chimney the other night? Our leg-up on the police and all that?"

"Yes, but we've shown it to Gilford, and he didn't seem much interested in it."

"Well, has that ever stopped you before?"

"Hmm… maybe you're right, even without the fragment itself, we could still go to London and question Thea's publisher about her latest book project. He's bound to know *something* about it."

"Exactly. And the thing is, *we still have it,* that snippet we found… Gilford clearly didn't look like he was interested in it, so it was easy enough for me to snatch it back from him. He didn't even notice, and I figured we might as well hang on to it."

"Really!?"

Darren rolled over to his low-slung writing desk, retrieved

the little snippet of singed paper and brought it over to his wife. "Here you are. Don't thank me."

"Wonderful!"

Delicately Daisy handled the fragment of typescript, held it close to her nose and sniffed up the tinge of charred paper. Stroking its surface with her fingertips, she thought she could feel where the letters had been embossed in neat rows by the type hammers. She was entranced. This felt so tangible and held so much promise!

"First we'll have to find out who Thea's publisher is," she said softly.

"That's more like it, you're sounding better already."

"You know what? Let's go down again and ask Sondra. Maybe she can get Thea's PA on the phone for us and find out."

Moments later their dear receptionist was telling them that she didn't even need to pester the famous author's PA to get this information, "If the poor woman has heard the news she'll be in a terrible state already." No, she said, they could do one better: look it up on the 'information superhighway'.

"What on earth is *that?*" Daisy cried.

"Don't you know about digital networks yet? It's also something we do with computers. Our hotel is connected to the 'World Wide Web' through a special phone line, so customers from all over the world can find us. It's really incredibly useful for business."

And before she'd completed her explanations for these old-fashioned ignoramuses, she'd already found the piece of information she'd been looking for, tapping briskly on the keyboard while she spoke: "Ah, here it is: Theodora Slayer's publishers are called 'Alexander and Custer'. Never heard of them... and there's a phone number. Do you want me to call them and make an appointment for you? I'll pretend to be the PA of the Dowager Countess of Haverford."

"It's sweet of you to offer, Sondra, but let's leave the countess out of this… I have a better idea. I'll call a good friend of mine, Beatrice, whose title is a great deal more impressive than mine and who knows everyone who's somebody in London. She'll know exactly to whom I should talk and will open the necessary doors for me."

"Sounds good. I wish *I* had more friends like that!"

So up to the flat they returned, with Darren positively chortling with glee in the lift, happy to see his darling wife back on the trail again, and looking forward to driving up to London. The couple owned a little Japanese car, adapted for a paraplegic with a special knob on the steering wheel and a kind of joystick for controlling the accelerator and the brakes, and Darren enjoyed being his wife's chauffeur very much. Besides, he was born and bred in London, and missed the great metropolis: the peace and quiet of the countryside could become a bit tedious sometimes. So he eagerly listened in on his wife's conversation with her old friend on the blower, as soon as they'd got back to the flat.

"Bee, darling? Daisy here, how are you? Listen… do you remember the play we wrote and performed in 1939, Murder of a Corpse? Yes, I know, *I* wrote most of it, basically, but anyway, after all these years there's actually been a *real* murder at Bottomleigh House, or so it appears to be, and I need your help… Yes, *of course* I'm putting my nose into an affair that's none of my business once again, but listen…"

And so it went on for a while. When she finally put the phone down, Daisy announced, "There you are, darling, did you hear that? Beatrice has invited us to Belmont House in Kensington. We can stay as long as we like."

"Hurray!"

Now that he was used to a manorial way of life, Darren much appreciated the possibility of combining the raw bustle of the metropolis with a particularly classy accommodation.

"She'll make an appointment for me with Mr Alexander, Thea's editor and publisher, and maybe we can fit in a visit to Johnny-John in Wormwood Scrubs as well."

Jonathan was Daisy's son, and Wormwood Scrubs was the prison where he was serving a life sentence for two gruesome murders. So it would be rather cosy to be able to combine one aspect of the family business with the other, Darren agreed. "And we mustn't forget to fill the Suzuki up on our way to London," he added.

The next morning they set out so early that Mister Kumar was still on duty behind the reception desk. He smiled broadly at them when he saw the comical spectacle of the blind 'lady of the manor' pushing her husband's wheelchair out of the lift, their luggage piled up high in his lap.

"Good morning, Mister Kumar!" Daisy exclaimed after he'd greeted her, "how are you? No worries, I hope?"

"I'm fine, Mrs Hayes, thank you. I suppose you managed to speak to your friends from the police about my little problem?"

"Oh yes, never fear, they were receptive to my plea and understanding about the whole situation, very understanding indeed."

"Good. I'm grateful to you for interceding in my favour."

"Don't even mention it, my dear."

They walked on towards the exit, and the night porter discreetly activated the automatic door opener for them. But even at this early hour their departure did not go unnoticed from Mister Robbins. He suddenly emerged from his living quarters, fully dressed, every inch the hotel manager, to the extent that it made Darren wonder if he ever changed into pyjamas. But Daisy wasn't aware of all that when the man challenged them forcefully.

72

"Good morning Mrs Hayes... Mr Miller," he called out to them, "fancy seeing you out and about at this early hour! Planning to travel, judging from the luggage? But didn't DCI Gilford edict clear instructions to the effect that *nobody* was to leave the premises for the duration of the ongoing investigation?"

"Good morning to you too, Mister Robbins. We were just leaving, indeed, we have some important business to attend to in London right now. As for the inspector's instructions, please keep in mind, first: that he said he couldn't *force* anyone to stay. Secondly: that his instructions were only meant for the *participants* of the Murder Convention, because thirdly, the dear man *definitely* told us he didn't consider Darren and me as suspects at all, and that the investigation was on hold for the time being anyway. So if you want to report our absconding to the police, feel free to do so, but I'm afraid they'll tell you that you're under a misapprehension... *Adios*, Mister Robbins."

And as the front door swung open, impelled by and electric actuator, and the glass door in front of it slid aside with a light hiss, Darren propelled them forward, and Daisy called out in a sing-song voice, "Thanks, Mister Kumar, Cheerio!"

III   A change of scene, a change of perspective

— 1 —

The publishing house was an impressive old place, located in a stately building on Gower Street in Bloomsbury, the traditional literary district of London. 'Alexander and Custer' carried all the weight of a centuries-old tradition, and Daisy thought she could hear it and smell it around her as they were led through the bustling upstairs offices by a young woman from reception, downstairs. Holding on to Beatrice's arm Daisy pricked up her ears, sniffed at the air, and felt she could perceive all the excitement attendant to the publishing trade, from muted telephone conversations, possibly with authors or printers, to the typical glue smell of freshly bound books. This was clearly a place where momentous tasks were being performed and significant literary productions prepared by a little army of competent and dedicated professionals.

Although the first thing dear Beatrice said when she introduced the publisher they had an appointment with was: "This is Rupert Alexander, Theodora Slayer's editor, and a dear old friend—we used to call him Pee-Wee Alexander."

"Oh please, Bee, have a heart!" the gentleman grumbled, "you know how I hate that nickname. Just because I wet my bed *once* when I was six years old!"

"Yes, but it was at the Spencers' and everybody was there."

"Well thanks for reminding me. But anyway, please be seated, what can I do for you ladies?"

Daisy now asked, "Did you hear what happened at the Murder Convention?"

"Yes, yes, Ruth Vine was so kind as to phone me yesterday and she told me all about it. She's also one of my authors, you understand. A charming lady."

"Very well, then I don't need to go into all the details of the case. The important thing to keep in mind is that we don't even know for sure if a crime has actually been committed, and that for the moment the police is not doing much to find out."

"Yes, annoying, that. And I'm grateful for the opportunity to speak to you, Mrs Hayes. As you live in the place where it happened, perhaps you can tell me more."

"Certainly. That's why I want to show you something that Mrs Vine probably doesn't know about."

Daisy opened her bag and retrieved the envelope containing the typescript fragment. She handed it over the desk behind which the publisher was sitting, and waited until he'd had the time to look at it.

"How extraordinary!" he exclaimed eventually, "where did you find this? Did *you* find it?"

"No, my husband who isn't blind spotted it. He noticed that some papers had been torn to pieces and burned in the library's fireplace. This is all that was left, and we concluded that it must be a piece of dialogue from the manuscript of a novel... Now, it could have been planted on the 'crime scene'

75

as part of a staged puzzle, or it could be an indication of something more sinister. In both cases the first question you need to answer is the same: does this belong to Thea? Do you recognize it?"

"As a matter of fact I do. 'Shrewd prey' definitely rings a bell. It must be from the novel Theodora has been working on lately, and I have a carbon copy of this same page right here in one of my drawers... Just a moment."

Daisy heard the muffled sliding of a few of the desk's drawers being pulled and shut one after the other, the flapping of stacks of papers being rummaged through, and finally a relieved muttering: "Here you are. Got it!" Beatrice, sitting next to her friend, squeezed her hand. Apparently the publisher leafed through a few pages, comparing them to the charred snippet he was holding next to them, until he found the place where the words 'shrewd prey' appeared, like he remembered. Then he handed the snippet and the flimsy carbon copy to Beatrice, who placed one on top of the other, and shifted it around until it fitted exactly, almost at the top of the page.

"Oh Daisy, if only you could see this, it's so *neat!*"

And she started reading the text out loud, still holding the fragment in place.

```
not unsatisfied altogether. The difficulties facing him made
him feel happy inside, rather in the way an old hunter would
feel on the track of a shrewd prey. Inspector Blondell looked
up at the girl standing in the doorway and asked her softly,
'My dear Mildred, tell me why you're getting so worked up.'
'Well, I simply don't even know myself. But while we're in no
hurry, I still feel it would take too long to explain.'
Blondell said no more but it occurred to him that she'd gone
through an awful lot since she'd disappeared.
```

"There you are," Daisy said after her friend had finished

reading, "hypothesis confirmed. Proof of concept. Isn't it wonderful?"

"Typical first draft prose," Rupert Alexander commented, "a bit rough around the edges. I have ten pages like that, carbon copies of something my dear Thea 'just banged out' on her typewriter. She's not one to write a synopsis, but always submits a new project in this form: a copy of the opening chapter, fresh from the anvil, so to speak. I approved the sample at once and told her to go right ahead with the novel."

"Can you confirm that the snippet we salvaged from the fireplace is from the original typescript, not the copy?"

"Absolutely. Although I'm twenty years her junior, Thea and I both belong to a generation that grew up with typewriters. She can bang out a whole novel on a machine without a pause, and I can certainly distinguish the darker, smudgy marks left by an ink ribbon from the more faded ones of a carbon copy. Nowadays writers use only computers, but in that respect she and I are still old school."

"Very well, and do you reckon that Thea would have finished the first draft of her new novel?"

"Yes, I expect so. She would be going over it by now, filling it with deletions and corrections in pencil, although I can see none of those on the fragment you found."

"And would she have been doing that during the Murder Convention?"

"Possibly. She can't leave it alone for one moment. I'd expect that even during an event like this, that she herself is organizing, she'd be working on the novel in her spare moments."

"All right. So: supposing she took the manuscript along, would there be a carbon copy of the rest of it, apart from the ten pages you have?"

"No, certainly not. Thea positively *hates* messing about with those carbon sheets and extra layers of lightweight paper..."

Rupert Alexander sighed deeply, and added, "I hope to God that I won't need the past tense to talk about her any time soon."

"I hope so too," Daisy answered softly, "but I'm afraid there's another thing Ruth Vine probably couldn't tell you, and that I heard directly from a police officer: the blood on the rug is Thea Slayer's... so it's not looking good. That's why I've taken on the task of investigating further on my own."

"I see... yes... then it's a good thing that you've come to me."

"Now what can you tell me about this new novel?"

Rupert Alexander told them all they needed to know about his star author's new book, synopsis or no synopsis. He'd discussed it at length with her after he'd read those first ten pages and given his blessing to the work in progress. The title Thea had in mind summed it up neatly in a few words: 'Tables Turned in Hell'. The story of a man who is wrongly accused of a crime he didn't commit, who spends his time in prison plotting his revenge, then breaks out, tracks down the real culprit and threatens to commit the same crime against him for which he has already been unjustly punished.

"A clever plot, as always in Thea's books," the publisher concluded.

"The story sounds somewhat familiar," Daisy remarked, "although I'm not sure why."

"There are two possible reasons for that. First, a similar plot is mentioned in E.C.R. Lorac's 'Death of an Author'."

"I've never heard of it."

"Then you may have heard about an infamous case that was in the news around 1980, almost fifteen years ago. A teenage girl from a wealthy family was kidnapped, and the desperate parents paid the ransom. But when the poor girl was released, it turned out she'd been repeatedly raped by her abductor. This man was identified and arrested, based on her testimony, but during his trial he kept proclaiming his innocence, and the counsel for the defence kept repeating that the case against him rested entirely on the dodgy testimony of a sixteen-year-old girl, full of holes and contradictions as it was. Nevertheless the accused, a man by the name of Milton, like the great poet, was sentenced to twenty years."

"Ah yes, *Greg* Milton, I heard it on the news at the time. It was quite a sensation... So Thea's new novel is a story of revenge based on this real-life case?"

"That's right. She changed the names, but her idea was to have the man who'd been wrongly sentenced break out from jail after a while and abduct the daughter of the real kidnapper, turning the tables on him. He threatens to rape her if he doesn't go to the police and make a full confession of what he did. But this wronged jailbird is an honourable man, and the young girl grows fond of him, despite the age difference, and she helps him take revenge on the police officer who arrested him at the time, and who in fact was her kidnapper. Their plot succeeds, and the real villain ends up behind bars in his turn. End of story."

"Very interesting indeed. And which girl would Mildred be, in the fragment Beatrice just read, the victim of the *first* abduction, or of the *second* one?"

"Well, I don't want to spoil the plot for you, but in the end Inspector Blondell finds out that Mildred is *both* these girls. The first time she was rather young and was manipulated into staging her own kidnapping by the handsome detective, so he could extort a ransom from her father. The second time she's a bit older, the jailbird having escaped only after a few years, and she's living with the man who put him behind bars, *pretending* to be his daughter. In the end Mildred helps Thea's habitual Scotland Yard sleuth Blondell to unmask his colleague, the swindling detective."

"All right, but this is just a story. Nothing proves that Greg Milton didn't do it, in the real world."

"Not as far as I know."

"Still, writing a novel along these lines about a real-life case is playing with fire a bit, no?"

"That's exactly what I told Thea from the beginning, but she assured me that the story she'd made up was too far removed from the facts to cause any problems, and that she would change all the names anyway. I had to accept her arguments, as I knew little about the case apart from what everyone had heard on the news... At any rate, Mildred is also a made-up name."

"Well, if Thea has been murdered, 'I changed the names' could well be the last words she uttered."

Sitting in his glass cubicle at the CID headquarters in Horsham, DCI Gilford was pondering some writerly conundrums of his own. How to do justice to a case like this without seeming callous or too eager to make it go away (which he was). How to avoid giving the impression that he blamed his superiors for this stalemate (which he did). It wouldn't do to write the truth: "We'll just have to wait for a corpse to turn up."

He'd made grateful use of some interesting ideas he'd pilfered from the Daily Bulletin these crazy writers published during their accursed Murder Convention. They seemed to have covered every possible explanation of what had happened pretty well. Apart from the possibility of a hoax, the most obvious solution was that Jack Reaper had killed Mrs Slayer, then made off with the body. But there was also the less obvious explanation that Mrs Slayer had killed Jack Reaper and wounded herself in the process. Or someone could have killed her and Reaper both, in which case the killer was still among the guests staying at the Manor Hotel.

Or perhaps Reaper and Mrs Slayer were lovers and had staged the whole thing in order to elope... etc, etc.

Sucking on the butt of his pencil the Chief reflected that it were in effect these accursed mystery writers themselves who proved to be rather callous and lacking any sense of responsibility. Although one of them (was it this Saccharine person again?) had contributed the astute observation that even if the police had made DNA profiles, they wouldn't have been of any use, as the identities of the victim and the killer were already known, and both had disappeared. The Chief intended to include that remark in his report.

Then there was Daisy Hayes. He'd used her inspired words in his concluding paragraph: "This is a wide-open case: it could be a staged puzzle, or a tragic accident, or it could be a carefully plotted murder attempt by someone who hopes to have devised the perfect crime." He couldn't for the life of him remember how this alleged perfect crime was supposed to have worked, exactly, but he remembered the formulation, and that it had sounded excellent at the time. It still looked good on paper... but what was the blind lady's game? Had she actually encouraged him to drop the case so she could pursue it herself, or had it been the other way round? All this was confusing, to put it mildly.

The Chief stared at his pencilled jottings for a while, then he looked over at his team on the other side of the glass partition. His men had gone back to their daily routine, which meant that they had little to do apart from a few light administrative tasks. However, young constable Hardy could always be relied on to transmute the most jumbled jottings from his boss's hand into a few pages of limpid prose with a little help from his computer, which he appeared to master with otherworldly proficiency. Excellent man, Hardy. Such a pity that he was a bit shy for a policeman, too unassuming, in contrast to Sergeant Mundie, who was rubbish with computers, but refreshingly assertive. The 'Sarge' could always be counted on to throw around his weight effectively, compensating a grating lack of subtlety with a surfeit of self-assurance...

Gilford sighed, went over his notes once more, making a few amendments left and right, and then he signalled constable Hardy to come and take them to be typed out.

— 2 —

"That went rather well, don't you think?" Daisy muttered while Beatrice guided her back to the waiting car.

"You can say that again. In fact we've made a roaring start on our investigation!" her old friend enthused as they clambered into the back of the Suzuki through its front door.

"Wouldn't it be something," Daisy sighed as she sank down in her seat, "if the burned manuscript turns out to hold the key to what happened to poor Thea?"

"Yes, but wouldn't it be even better if she just shows up again and it all turns out to be a hoax?"

"Of course! That would be absolutely lovely, but I still feel it's not likely."

"No, all things considered, maybe not."

Darren turned around from the driver's seat before starting the car. "Let me guess, Daisy was completely in her element in there, as usual, and was absolutely brilliant."

"Right you are, my dear. Pee-Wee even told her that if she ever started writing whodunnits of her own, she should come to him with her first manuscript. Daisy is really on top of her game!"

"D'you hear that, precious? You've got yourself a publisher already, I knew it... And where do we go now?"

"Well, Bee, your friend couldn't tell us much about the

Greg Milton case, but I know exactly who could. Do you remember Bernard Thistlehurst?"

"Bernard! Of course! I haven't met him for ages. Let's go and pick his brains."

"My idea exactly."

As they drove off Beatrice giggled from sheer excitement and relish. The truth of the matter was that living on your own at Belmont House in the poshest section of Kensington could be rather tedious sometimes. Since her parents had passed away poor Bee had become something of an 'impoverished aristocrat', due to the outlandish death duties she'd had to pay. And the taxes on her holdings and capital gains were pure murder, but she was too well-bred to even mention her financial problems. On top of that, there was no live-in staff left at Belmont, no butler, cook or gardener worth mentioning (you had independent 'caterers' and 'landscaping services' nowadays, but they cost dearly). And when all was said and done, the thing she missed most was the old family Bentley and its even older chauffeur, who'd long since retired. Beatrice couldn't drive, she'd never needed to learn, therefore tootling around London in the tiny Suzuki with Darren as a faithful chauffeur was an undiluted treat.

And the place where they were headed, in contrast to Alexander and Custer's premises, was not only accessible for wheelchair users, but had even been especially laid out and fitted up for their convenience. No carpeting, no rugs, and all the inner doors removed from the top-floor flat of an extraordinary Victorian mansion block on the Chelsea Embankment, right across from Battersea Park. From up there you had a beautiful view on the Thames, looking over and in between the Embankment's plane trees. The flat was directly accessible from the street by way of a lift, just like at home. Bernard was an old acquaintance, and also a wheelchair-bound paraplegic, which was why Darren was really looking forward to visiting his place. Hopefully he would be home, and glad to see them. It was going to be a surprise visit, on the spur of the moment, so you could never be sure.

But when he opened the door for them the elderly paralytic seemed quite happy. Daisy was an old flame, and he was an erstwhile crack investigator from the Metropolitan Police, so these two still delighted in each other's company. Within minutes of their arrival they'd all settled in the central area of the living room with G&Ts at hand. The two ladies were seated in extremely low-slung armchairs, and put their drinks beside them on the floor, while Bernard and Darren towered over them from their wheelchairs, a slightly comical setup reminiscent of a Charlie Chaplin film.

"So to what do I owe the pleasure?" Bernard Thistlehurst exclaimed amiably, and to Darren he said, "how do you like the manor life so far, my friend?

"It's okay... it grows on you."

"We've come to pick your brains about an old case," Daisy added, "and I can't deny that we want to take advantage of your encyclopaedic knowledge of criminal records from the past. But first I'll need to tell you about the case that's bothering us right now, I don't think you would have heard about it yet."

"Well I'm all ears, my dear, and delighted if I may be of assistance in any way I can."

And Daisy outlined the particulars of the events that had taken place at the Manor Hotel with her signature fluency and effectiveness, including Darren's find, and what Thea's publisher had just told them. When she'd finished, the old detective exclaimed, "What a baffling case indeed, my dear! I don't understand it... yet."

"You mean the underlying message?"

"Precisely. If a murder has taken place, *what is the murderer trying to tell us?*"

"My biggest worry is that he or she is only trying to confuse us in order to get away with it. This could be the ideal setup to commit the perfect crime: the victim and the killer both vanish, and there's no way of telling who is which."

"And that might be all there is to it, you're right."

"And the biggest question is, where does the *manuscript* I just told you about fit in? Is it part of a devilish plot, or does it on the contrary indicate that there's something entirely different going on?"

"I see. So the lady who might or might not have come to harm was writing a novel about the criminal case for which Greg Milton was sentenced to twenty years... in 1980 or thereabouts... yes, I distinctly remember, it was called the Bowen case, after the victim, Tilly Bowen, who was sixteen at the time of the facts. May I have a look at the snippet you and Darren found in the fireplace?"

Daisy took the precious talisman from her handbag and presented it to her old friend with an outstretched arm. Bernard wheeled over and took hold of it. He fingered it for a while and studied it, feeling its power. He exchanged knowing glances with the two other sighted people present, and muttered under his breath: "Extraordinary. So this is all there is left from that manuscript?"

"Yes, but we've just been shown ten pages of a carbon copy, onto which this fragment fitted exactly, as I said... Now what do you make of Theodora Slayer's treatment of the story: that the detective who arrested the kidnapper had in fact staged the girl's abduction and framed someone else for it in order to collect the ransom?"

"A rather clever plot, I must admit. The accused would have denied any knowledge of the ransom money, making himself all the more suspect, and as soon as he was found guilty and sentenced, the real culprit could enjoy the fruits of his crime undisturbed. However, I find the story unlikely, all in all. The case against Greg Milton was rock-solid, precisely because the man who'd handled it was such a competent and respected CID detective. He'd done an excellent job."

Bernard couldn't remember his name any more, but that was beside the point. He did recall that the police officer who'd found the kidnapped girl and arrested her abductor had become a hero overnight and a national celebrity for a short while. Everybody had been in awe of the brilliant sleuthing that had led to such a spectacular result. The raid on the derelict hut in the woods where the girl had been held was seen as a heroic intervention, and the national press had lapped it up.

"Not necessarily a propitious precondition for a fair trial," Daisy remarked, "and it would fit Thea's story quite well: the brilliant detective is the real culprit and that's precisely why he can get away with it."

"I'll grant you that, in theory, my dear. And if I remember correctly, the counsel for the defence protested strongly that the case leaned too heavily on the testimony of a sixteen-year-old girl that they couldn't cross-examine because she was still a minor. She wasn't even allowed to be present at the trial. But then again, the personality of the accused didn't help either."

"You *do* seem to remember a lot… so what was wrong with the accused?"

To start with, Greg Milton had done little to exculpate himself during the trial, Bernard explained, except by strenuously proclaiming his innocence without providing any particulars, as much as his counsel had attempted to make him go into the details of his side of the story. It became clear that the man was a small-time crook, the smart offspring of an underprivileged family who could have done well for himself if only he'd been kept in check and encouraged more at school as a boy, but who instead had applied his wits to a

86

career of petty crime, graduating from shoplifting to armed robbery of a few petrol stations.

"Very sad... At any rate that was the picture painted by the prosecution. When he was put away for that kidnapping, he at least was already familiar with prison life and knew how to make the best of it, or so one could hope."

"Is he still behind bars?"

"I expect so, yes, but you'd have to ask the prison authorities for his precise whereabouts. Maybe my good friend Collins could help you out with that."

"If you could ask him on my behalf, that would be lovely... but first one more question: did Greg Milton actually *rape* poor Tilly Bowen? Rupert Alexander seemed to think that he was put away for rape as well."

"No, I don't think that is the case, I can't recall that there was question of anything like that. But again, Collins could tell us more."

"Well, I suppose Thea's publisher must have conflated the story she made up with what he remembered of the trial... But anyway, could you get Collins on the phone for me right now?"

"Of course. You don't like to let the grass grow under your feet, do you?"

Collins was an old acquaintance who'd been instrumental in putting Daisy's son Jonathan behind bars for two gruesome murders a few years before. At the time young Collins had been a mere detective constable, whom Bernard had taken under his wing, but meanwhile he'd become a full inspector at New Scotland Yard's CID, while his former boss had retired. At any rate a very useful contact inside the Metropolitan Police.

He was delighted to hear his former mentor's voice on the phone, and even more to hear that 'Mrs Hayes' was back in the picture, on the trail of a murder case again. "Sir, please get her on the line, I want to talk to her myself... Anything I can do to help!"

So Daisy had to explain once more the events that had so dramatically marred the Murder Convention, and put to him the burning question she was dying to ask: where was Greg Milton being held, and would it be possible to talk to him?

"My dear Mrs Hayes," DC Collins answered fondly, "I could find out in a jiffy and even arrange an appointment for you to visit the man, but you do realize that if he has been behind bars for almost fifteen years, he can have nothing to do with the disappearance of the two participants of this bizarre club at the hotel where you live?"

"Yes, yes, you're absolutely right, Collins. I guess I'm just doggedly following the only trail we have to find out where it will lead us. We need to know more about the Bowen case, but also about Theodora Slayer's involvement with it. She was playing with fire... Did she visit Greg Milton in prison and talk to him about her project? How did he react if she did? The only way to find out is to ask *him*."

"All right, sounds reasonable. I'll take an early lunch break so I can ask around on my own... You know, I was a great admirer of Kevin Tyler at the time, that's the detective who handled the case. I was just starting out as a bobby on the beat, he was on the news, his picture everywhere, and my young colleagues and I just *dreamed* of emulating his exploits... I'll get back to you in a moment."

As Daisy cradled the receiver she sighed: "How lovely to hear Collins's voice again, he hasn't changed one bit."

"Apart from his rank, that is," Bernard remarked, "that boy has made a stellar career, and I'm proud of him."

"As you should. You saw his potential from the very beginning, didn't you? Now could you give me his number at the Yard, so I can write it down in Braille? It might come in useful."

Daisy retrieved her pocket-size Braille slate from her handbag, and Bernard watched with great interest how she punched the numbers he dictated into a little card with a special stylus. He knew that she had to put together the Braille figures backwards and mirrored, so the embossed dots would be legible on the other side of the card. Weren't all blind people who could do such a thing incredibly clever?

When the phone rang again on the low coffee table in front of her, Daisy picked it up at once and Collins on the other side of the line told her that he'd spoken to his contact in Her Majesty's prison service, but that unfortunately Greg Milton had recently been released for good behaviour after serving two-thirds of his sentence. He was a free man, and no one knew his whereabouts, apart from the parole board, maybe, but there was no way to get more information, except if an official police investigation was opened against him.

"Well there's no question of that, obviously," Daisy replied, "and I'm happy for the man. There's no 'unfortunately' about it."

"I only meant unfortunately for *you*, Mrs Hayes," Collins chuckled, "but there's another piece of information that might interest you. You'll never guess *where* Greg Milton served his sentence during all those years: at Wormwood Scrubs, just like your Jonathan!"

"Well that certainly *is* something, yes... Who knows, maybe my boy will be able to tell me more about the man. If I call the warders' office right now I might even be able to visit him this afternoon."

There was a short silence, and then Daisy added, "Speaking of which, this Kevin Tyler you mentioned, do you know him at all? Do you think I could talk to him as well?"

"Ah, I'm afraid I can't help you there, no, Mrs Hayes. You see, when I started here at the CID a few years ago he'd already left the service for quite some time, so I never met him personally. I asked around about him at the time, when I started, but all the colleagues who'd known him told me they'd lost touch with him after he'd gone... therefore, same story, whereabouts unknown."

"That's a pity, Constable... Oh! listen to me, I'm still calling you *Constable*."

"That's all right. Makes me feel a lot younger."

— 3 —

Beatrice had never been to Wormwood Scrubs before, she knew it by name, but had never even seen the building from the outside. Therefore the next stop on their quest held some fresh excitement for Daisy's old friend. After the two 'girls' had clambered out of the Suzuki, Bee turned around and took in the forbidding, medieval-looking building, with its turrets left and right of the main entrance, before she gave her arm to Daisy. She was told to make for a side entrance around the corner, where a number of visitors, mostly women, were waiting in line for the security check.

"You can leave me now, darling, only one visitor at a time allowed, and the other ladies will take good care of me from here. You go back to the car and Darren will take you to his favourite pub... meet you here in an hour."

"All right. Say hello to Jonathan for me... that is, if he still knows who I am."

"Oh I'm sure he does... I will."

Moments later the mother and her son were reunited in the visitor's room. They were not allowed to embrace or even hug, but they'd never been demonstrative with their affection anyway, at least Jonathan had not. He gave his mother a peck on the cheek in passing before he sat down across from her at the table, and she briefly squeezed his arm in return.

The warders always let it pass if you left it at that.

"Why did you come *today*, Mum? This is not our *normal* visiting day!"

"I know. I hope you don't mind, darling. I promise I'll come back on the normal day as well, if that's all right with you."

"We'll see. You *know* I hate surprises."

"Well sorry about that, but today at least I won't be pestering you with questions about how you're doing and so on…"

"Good. I hate *that* as well."

"Today I need your help in a case I'm investigating. Have you ever heard about a man named Greg Milton? He served his sentence here until recently, or so I was told."

"Old Greg? Sure I remember him. But what do you want from him? He was a good mate of mine before he left, and I'm not going to *rat* on him."

"Of course not, no need for that, and I'm delighted to hear that he's your friend…"

"You always say that, like I couldn't be *anyone's* friend, normally."

"Well, just tell me nice things about your mate, will you? I heard he always denied that he had anything to do with the kidnapping they put him away for… did you ever hear him talk about it?"

"Of course… a lot… that's why we became friends in the first place. Everybody always says they didn't do it, and no one ever believes them. But with Greg it was different, he had a *good reason*, and I *listened* to his argument, and I told him he had a point. So he liked that."

"See? You're already being helpful. That's the case I'm investigating, and I'm only trying to prove he didn't do it. So what was it? What was the good point he made?"

"He said it was probably the cop who handled his case that actually *did it*. Everybody was banging on about how

91

brilliant he was, a real hero, it was in the news and all over the papers. But isn't that a bit suspicious? Greg said. The guy knew *exactly* where to go looking for the girl in a little hut in the middle of the woods. What if he had brought her there *himself* to start with?"

"Valid point! But how can you prove a thing like that? I'm sure Greg Milton told all this to his counsel as well, but there was probably not much they could do about it."

"Exactly. That's what Greg told me too. And then he said it's no use getting all het up about it anyway, and that his plan was to get a sentence reduction for good behaviour as soon as possible. All you need to do is to become a model convict."

"Sounds good. And apparently it worked!"

"Yes. And what he did to get that reduction was quite simple, actually. He started writing books. And he became a custodian of the prison library. As a volunteer at first. He did it in his spare time. But later he was *seconded* fulltime, because he was incredibly good at it."

The problem, Jonathan explained to his mother, was that Her Majesty's prisons *never throw away a book*. So the prison libraries have a huge number of old books, at least a hundred years old, and *nobody* reads those anymore. In the old days a lot of charities would donate *religious* books to prisons for the 'rehabilitation' of the inmates, Jonathan expounded somewhat pompously, and *unis* like Oxford and Cambridge would donate a lot of *classics* from Ancient Rome and Greece for their 'improvement'... Now, good old Greg turned out to be a genius at finding the most *juicy parts* in all those antique books, the sexiest chapters of the Old Testament, say, or the endless martyrizing of the Christian Saints, especially those virtuous *virgins!* and all the shenanigans of the Roman emperors. He would put little strips of paper between the pages at the most exciting parts, as *bookmarks*, see, and the other inmates started borrowing all those old classics from the prison library really greedily, like on a regular basis, to the great satisfaction of the head warder.

"And in his spare time Greg Milton started writing books of his own, also exciting and sexy, with plenty of pretty girls in each story, about a private eye in Ancient Rome who solves *gruesome* murders that always turn out to have been committed on orders from powerful and *depraved* politicians, you know... And guess what? Greg even found a publisher who actually *printed* his books. He must be making buckets of money with them right now."

"Well-well, what a story," Daisy enthused at the end of this exposition, "talk about mixing business with pleasure! And it got him out of prison too."

"Yes, Mum, and now I want to try and do the same. I'm already a volunteer for distributing and collecting the books on loan in my spare time, and I'm hoping to get seconded to the library too, one day, just like old Greg. We have all his novels in our collections, and they're a great success with the inmates."

Meanwhile, what with Jonathan's lengthy digressions about Cleopatra, various virgin martyrs, the Song of Solomon and the Queen of Sheba, time had flown by and already the visiting hour was coming to an end. The head warder cautioned the visitors that they should "wind it up, please!" and prepare to leave. Daisy quickly reached over the table and squeezed her son's hand.

"I'm so glad to hear that you're doing well, Johnny-John. You seem a lot more relaxed than you've been in a long time. Keep your spirits up, do you hear me? I hope it will work out in the library, and maybe I should let Darren read one of your friend's books to me so we can discuss it the next time I visit, yes? Let me buy one for you. Do you know the name of the publisher? And which one would you like to have?"

"Well, if I remember correctly Greg's publisher is called Hercules, and I want you to buy me 'Farewell, Mea Culpa'. A bit funny, for the title of a book, but I hope you can remember it. I liked it a lot, and you must absolutely read it too."

"I will. 'Farewell, Mea Culpa', by Greg Milton…"

"Actually, no. Don't ask me why, but Greg's name as a writer is Lee Quincy. Can you remember that?"

"*Lee Quincy…* Sure. I will."

Compared to 'Alexander and Custer', Lee Quincy's publisher was a different kettle of fish. Beatrice had to look up the number and address in the yellow pages of a phone directory in a pub. Then Daisy called from that same pub and winkled an appointment out of the man who answered the phone, turning on her most enticing tone of voice. She'd sounded at least thirty-five years younger, Darren thought. That, and the fact that she'd subtly hinted at the *possibility* of some lucrative business dealings in a not too distant future, had done the trick. Then they drove over to an anonymous industrial estate, roaming for a while through a maze of identical streets, half lost, Darren and Bee desperately looking for a hoarding with the name 'Hercules Publishing' on it. At last they found the place in a derelict side alley with a lot of non-descript, shuttered sheds, and this one lowslung warehouse turned out to be the firm's seat.

There was only one man on the premises, apparently the manager and sole employee, but he received them amiably enough in a glass cubicle at the side of a vast stockroom where he'd been packing stacks of books into cardboard boxes for shipping.

"Mister Wilson," Daisy said sweetly as soon as they were seated, Darren parked right next to her and Bee sitting on the other side, "my husband and I have recently made the acquaintance of one of your authors, Lee Quincy, who spoke very highly of you as his publisher. As it happens we are permanent residents of the Manor Hotel in Bottomleigh, where the Murder Convention is taking place right now. I don't know if you heard about it, but it must have been quite an honour for your star author to get himself invited there."

"Yes, Lee and I were rather astonished when he received that letter from none other than the great Theodora Slayer herself… The thing is, to tell you the truth, Lee is not one of the best-selling mystery authors of the country, and he's certainly not supposed to be a member of the Top Ten Club. As you can see for yourself, or rather your husband will tell you, *we're* not a big publishing house, and humorous historical mysteries are our speciality, but it's a niche product at best. Nevertheless, Lee and I turned out to be a perfect match, as I was able to connect him with a small but devoted readership for his Philippus Marlovius stories. Everybody satisfied, but hardly enough to get yourself invited to such an event by the doyenne of the British mystery."

"Lee Quincy wasn't acquainted with her before this invitation?"

"Not to my knowledge, no. I mean, they don't hang out in the same circles at all."

"All right, there's clearly something of a mystery there as well… Have you heard about what *happened* at the Murder Convention?"

"Oh yes, Lee phoned me the other day and told me about it. He seemed to think that it was all a staged game, which he found a bit silly, and he was quite amused by the fact that he was the only person there who actually had an ironclad alibi for the time when reportedly everyone had heard 'a scream in the night'… Now, apart from all that, Mrs Hayes, you were hinting at some business matters on the phone, so what can I do for you?"

"Business matters... yes... just before I called you I was visiting my son at *Wormwood Scrubs*, where he's serving time at Her Majesty's disposal, as they say. Do you know the place?"

"I know it by name, but I can't say I've ever been there."

"Well, during my visit, my son Jonathan was telling me about Lee Quincy... he was telling me... he was quite excited about it... *that they have all his books in their library!* And Jonathan's a great fan of Philippus Marlovius's adventures."

While Daisy tried to draw out her quarry in this manner, Darren scrutinized the publisher's expression to gauge his reaction... discreetly, mind you. But if the poker-faced Mister Wilson was aware of his writer's real identity, he certainly didn't let on. Likewise when she'd asked if his protégé knew Thea Slayer.

"I think it's wonderful for prison inmates like my son to be able to lose themselves into some exciting adventures in Ancient Rome, you know. It has nothing to do with the grim reality of their predicament, and at the same time it's extremely instructive and educational for them... How many books has Lee Quincy written in the series so far?"

"Seven, but there are more to come, it's an ongoing project."

"Very well! What I have in mind is to donate those books to as many of Her Majesty's prisons as possible. I'd like you to draw up a budgeted proposal to that effect, as I have no idea how many prison libraries there are in our country, and how much it would cost altogether to provide them with these excellent books. Could you look into it? Here is my business card—the one for sighted people—so you can get in touch with me as soon as you have the information."

"Great, but we're talking about a major operation here, I don't even have that many copies of the series in stock right now."

"There's no hurry. Let's start with a few major prisons at first, and expand our range over time, shall we? My son's favourite is the first volume, 'Farewell, Mea Culpa', but I haven't read it yet—or my husband hasn't had the opportunity to read it to me. Do you happen to have a copy for us?"

"Of course."

"I'll pay for it."

"Absolutely not. It's on the house."

"Did you just winkle a free copy of one of his books out of that poor man in there?" Darren asked reproachfully as they went back to the car.

"Yes, but don't worry, I *really* intend to launch that charity I outlined to him, so he'll get my custom all right, in the end. Although I must admit that I thought it up on the spur of the moment."

"Never mind about that," Beatrice remarked, "what I find totally baffling right now, is *how could Thea possibly have discovered Lee Quincy's true identity?* Or didn't she? I'm a bit confused."

As he opened the car door and his wife assisted him to climb inside, Darren told Daisy, "At least his *publisher* doesn't seem to know a thing about it, in spite of all the trouble you took to trip him up."

"And even if he does, he's duty-bound not to let on. But anyway, in Thea's case it's quite obvious, really. She *didn't* find out who Lee Quincy was, for the simple reason that she went looking for *Greg Milton* in the first place. She must have visited him in prison when she started researching the Bowen case. It stands to reason. She wanted to hear his side of the story... and then she found out that he was writing mysteries too."

"Oh... right... it *is* quite simple," Bee had to admit.

"Maybe Thea read his first novel and gave him the address

97

of Hercules Publishing, knowing that 'humorous historical mysteries' were their speciality. At any rate she knew about his pseudonym."

"All right, so where do we go from here?"

"I'd like to know more about the reasons why Thea invited Quincy to the Murder Convention, even though he is definitely not a member of the Top Ten Club. It seems a bit... *cavalier* for a finicky old lady like her. And I know exactly who might shed some light on this."

"You don't say."

"Thea's PA, that's who. I don't even know her name, but Sondra could give us her phone number. If we hurry, we can still catch her at work."

So Darren rushed them back to the pub from where his darling wife had phoned Quincy's publisher. The telephone there lived inside an open, sound-proof cubicle fixed to the wall right next to the toilets, so you could at least talk undisturbed, and allow a couple of eager helpers to listen in.

Sondra was at her post as expected, and not only gave Daisy the number she required, but also recommended that she identify herself as 'the Dowager Countess of Haverford', because then Thea's PA would know at once who she was speaking with. "Her name is Miss Wesley by the way, and your title made a big impression on her and her boss," Sondra added.

Miss Wesley picked up the phone at once and opened the conversation with the words: "Theodora Slayer's office, good afternoon! What can I do for you?"

Then, as soon as Daisy had introduced herself she cried, "Oh! what a relief to hear your voice, Milady! I've been waiting for news from the police, but I haven't heard from them for ages! They don't seem to understand the seriousness of the situation at all. I'm worried sick!"

"So you don't think this whole affair could have been

staged for the benefit of the convention participants?"

"Certainly not! If that were the case I would be the first one to know about it, for the simple reason that I would have had to organize the whole thing to start with."

"But it came as a complete surprise?"

"Absolutely! And the police appear to be washing their hands of the whole matter. That's why I'm so glad to hear from you. Are you carrying on the investigation on your own, Milady? What on earth is going on? Please tell me that my dear, talented Mrs Slayer is still alive!"

The poor woman sounded genuinely distraught, and Daisy reflected that she seemed to think any member of the gentry, as she saw it, could solve any problem for you at the drop of a hat. "Listen, Miss Wesley," she answered softly, "I'm afraid it's not looking good. I was told in confidence by a police officer that the blood they found on the rug is indeed Mrs Slayer's, and as there's not much they can do about it for the time being, I've decided to launch into a little investigation of my own, like you say. That's why I need your help."

She started by asking the anxious assistant when she'd last spoken to her employer, and how she'd sounded. Miss Wesley reported that Thea had phoned her just before 'closing time' on the day she'd disappeared. She'd sounded quite happy, making good progress on the revision of her new novel's first draft.

"So she kept you posted on her work in progress, did she? And have you already read any part of that first draft?"

"No. Mrs Slayer keeps her unfinished creations strictly to herself. I would be delighted to type anything she wants on the computer for her, no matter how rough it might still seem in her own eyes, but there's nothing doing, she's rather protective and superstitious about showing unfinished work to anyone... except Mr Alexander, but that's different... However, she *likes* to confide in me about how her labours are progressing."

"I see. So you're exactly the right person to ask *how long* she'd been working on 'Tables Turned in Hell'."

"You know about that too, do you Milady? You even know the *title* of her new book, which is a tightly-kept secret! Well, she's been working on it for about a year, but the original idea came to her a few years ago, say two or three. That's when she took an interest in the infamous Bowen case for the first time."

"And that's when she went to Wormwood Scrubs and talked to Greg Milton."

"Exactly. Oh, how clever you are, Milady!"

"Now, I've just heard from his publisher that Lee Quincy isn't a best-selling author at all, not in such a way that he could join the Top Ten Club. So how come Mrs Slayer invited him to her convention anyway?"

"*'Her* convention' is precisely the right wording, Milady. My employer can be very proprietary and wilful about the event she initiated many years ago... In fact she invited Mr Quincy against all the rules to get rid of another, more legitimate member, Mr Simon. Perhaps you've heard about George Simon's recent novel, 'The Poisoned Pen Affair'. It's a cruel spoof on Mrs Slayer's work, and a huge success at her expense, poor thing... So, to get even, she shamelessly transferred his membership to Mr Quincy, or Milton, and good riddance."

"All right, that explains it."

"They've become great friends, you know. Mrs Slayer took Mr Milton's protestations of innocence at face value for the sake of a good story to start with, but the more they discussed what had actually happened, the more she came to believe that he's been unjustly condemned... Especially after his release, when they visited the hut in the woods together, the place where the police found Tilly Bowen. That's when my employer had her real *brain throb*, as she called it, and thought up the character of Mildred Monroe. Mrs Slayer gave me to understand, in confidence, that in the book she's a manipulative young creature, not as innocent as she appears to be at first, to say the least."

"How intriguing! So Greg Milton took her to the hut? He knew where it was?"

"Yes, he'd been there once before, he said, he'd been *lured* to the place with a promise of easy money, and the police was lying in wait, and *pounced* on him as soon as he showed up. That's what he told Mrs Slayer."

"All right, but what has the hut got to do with the brain throb about Tilly Bower?"

"I can't tell you more about that, Milady. The only thing she told me was that she *saw something* there."

— 4 —

The next morning they set off for the small town of Dorking, in the Surrey Hills, not far to the south of London. Darren, with Beatrice by his side, was closely following a police car with detective Collins at the wheel, and his old friend Daisy in the passenger seat next to him. A cosy little expedition. Bee muttered, "what are those two up to," and wondered out loud what they hoped to find in that hut in the woods after almost fifteen years.

"Beats me," Darren said, " but you have to admit that when our Daise is on a trail, you're in for a rough ride, and you're definitely going somewhere… and 'constable' Collins knows that all too well, so here we are."

In the front car the detective inspector was also reflecting out loud.

"As it happens, our conversation yesterday set me think-

101

ing, and in the afternoon I spent a couple of hours going through the records of the Bowen case... a good thing we're having a rather quiet time at the CID right now... and I'd already concluded that I wouldn't mind having a look at the famous hut in the woods myself. So picture my surprise when you called me this morning and proposed the same thing!"

"Sorry about pestering you, but I just find it too intriguing. I went to boarding school in this region as a young girl, before the war. And then the idea that Greg Milton was *lured* to that hut! Do you think there could be something in it?"

"It's not mentioned in the records, the suspect certainly didn't include this story in his testimony."

"Well I've been thinking about that all night, almost. What if he was offered 'easy money' to *kill* someone? It would explain both why he wasn't told *who* made the offer, and why he couldn't tell the police about it."

"Yes, not bad," Collins admitted, "you can always be counted on to come up with a fresh look on things... but in the end we'll just have to ask Mister Quincy himself... if the police reopens the case."

"And if they don't, *I* will, don't you worry."

Collins smiled. "For the moment it's the only reason why the CID is bothering to look into this again. In the end I'll have to write a lengthy report about whether or not there are any grounds for reopening the case: that's the price I'll have to pay for our little caper."

"Well I'm grateful that you're willing to put yourself out for me like this."

"Ah, for old times' sake, you know. In the past no one has ever regretted listening to you."

From Dorking they took a smaller road into the hills, following precise instructions Collins had taken over from the

Bowen case's files. He didn't know the region at all, he told Daisy, but the roads were numbered, and by the time they had to leave those he would be relying on a hand-drawn map that he'd also found in the archives.

"We're not far from Horsham and Crawley, aren't we?" she answered, "so if you get lost you can always ask Darren. We've been roaming this countryside by car on a daily basis since we moved to Bottomleigh House, he knows the region quite well by now."

"Well Horsham is much further down south, though, but I'm sure we'll find the place all right. Thanks for the offer anyway."

They continued their journey, single-mindedly following the instructions along country lanes that seemed to become narrower and narrower, veering off at right angles into alleys and tracks that became increasingly bumpy and difficult to drive on. "Are Darren and Bee still behind us?" Daisy asked nervously.

"Yes, don't worry... and we're almost there... but we're in the middle of the woods now and I'm not sure your husband will be able to use his wheelchair when we reach the hut."

"Don't worry, he'll stay in the car if he has to; he does that often enough when he's taking me places."

Finally they arrived at the end of a rather overgrown drive that came to a dead end tantalizingly close to a solitary cottage. Daisy could hear thorny twigs scratching the car's sides as they crept forward. By the time Collins announced that a small 'structure' had come into view ahead of them, they couldn't drive any further.

"This is the only 'hut' far and wide in this nick of the woods, so this must be it," Collins concluded, and he added that the terrain was fairly muddy too on account of recent showers, so what he'd just said about the wheelchair certainly applied.

"No worries, I'll put it to Darren, but it's for him to decide. Perhaps Bee will want to stay in the car too, to spare her fancy footwear… You and me, I guess, are at least wearing sensible shoes."

And that is how DI Collins ended up making his way towards the derelict cottage through the bushes, with only his blind old friend tagging doggedly along behind him, holding on to a bottom flap of his jacket. "Do you reckon that anyone lives here at the moment?" she asked.

"It seems rather abandoned, but I did spot some fresh tyre marks in the mud of the drive when we arrived. So someone has been here recently, but it could be the landlord or some holidaymakers who rented the place recently. I'll have to enquire."

During their drive Collins had told Daisy that the 'hut in the woods' still belonged to the same landowner as at the time of the Bowen case, and that it was not permanently occupied, but more like a rental weekend residence.

"In fact this is not at all what I expected," Collins added as they stopped at the front door and he rapped on it vigorously, "the *hut* mentioned in all the reports turns out to be a perfectly comfortable-looking cottage! The only thing that meets the grim picture that was suggested, is that it is really situated in a darkish forest, in the middle of nowhere."

They waited for some time, but nothing stirred inside the house.

"Maybe that is precisely what struck Theodora Slayer too, when she came here with Greg Milton: that the place where Tilly Bowen had been 'sequestrated' was in fact a quite comfortable holiday cottage. Hence her brainwave that Tilly could have been implicated in a plot set up by her own father."

"Yes, possibly. But what do we do now? There's clearly nobody at home."

"Well, how about we walk around the house and you take

a peep through each and every window? For starters I'd like to know if the place is a mess inside, or if it looks like it's being taken good care of."

"All right, now that we've come all this way…"

"Exactly."

They proceeded along a flagstone path to the back of the cottage, and Collins dutifully peered inside through every window they encountered, taking in a poorly-lit interior that seemed peaceful and cosy enough, as far as he could make out. There were even some French windows that gave access to the back garden from the living room. The heavy curtains were drawn, but a chink that had been carelessly left between them let through a little light and allowed a restricted view of the gloomy space behind.

"Good God!" Collins suddenly exclaimed, "there's somebody lounging on the couch in there!"

"Really!?"

The detective rapped on a pane of the French window quite forcibly, but there was no reaction, apparently, and he said, "Now I have the right to break in. This person might need help!"

Then, looking left and right for the best place to force his way in, he noticed that the window next to the one he'd been peering through wasn't locked, the handle of its latch mechanism in a vertical position instead of horizontal. So he simply pushed it open, took Daisy's hand, and they stepped inside through the curtains.

"Hello? Can you hear me? Are you all right?" he cried as he bent over the motionless body leaning against the backrest of the couch. He stretched his arm and put his finger on the side of the neck to check for a pulse. "Oh Lord, he's dead!"

"Is it a man?" Daisy asked. She hadn't said a word yet, only listening intently to what was happening.

105

"A man, yes, and his body is already rigid, so he has been dead for no less than four hours... it must have happened last night."

"We came too late!"

"At least we didn't come here for nothing... but wait a minute, I think I know this man!"

Collins stepped back to the windows and opened the curtains wide with a mighty swish. Then he stepped over to the seated body again and had another look.

"Exactly what I thought. I only know him from photos, but I think this must be *Kevin Tyler*, the former CID detective. How on earth did *he* end up dead in this place?"

Moments later they were back where they'd left the cars. Collins 'called in the troops' on the police frequency of his patrol vehicle while Daisy joined Darren and Bee in the Suzuki and told them the sensational news. They heard the detective inspector giving instructions through the radio: "Get in touch with our colleagues in Surrey, will you, they'll escort you to the crime scene... I need an ambulance and a forensics team pronto... never mind from which division, we've got a *homicide* on our hands... strangulation, by the look of it."

"Good God!" Beatrice exclaimed, "once again you seem to attract this kind of thing like a magnet, Daise."

"No I do not! I didn't ask for this, you know, I just followed the trail, that's all."

"And you didn't even get to *see* the corpse," Darren remarked, "anything familiar about the smells in there?"

"No, now that you mention it, I have no idea who this is. I mean, I don't expect that I would know anything about Kevin Tyler anyway, but we must make sure that you get to have a look at him too."

Collins joined them by the side of their car when he'd finished making arrangements, and he told them, "The police are on their way, this has become an official murder investigation if I know anything about it, so what shall we do now? Do you think you can find your way back to the main road on your own, Darren?"

"Yes, that I can, but do you *want* us to leave? We'd rather stick around, you know, and see what happens."

"All right, suit yourself, but that's going to take an awful lot of time…"

"The thing is," Daisy intervened, "I'd like Darren, and Beatrice too if she wants, to have a look at the corpse so that they can describe what they see to me. That's how we operate, normally. Darren and Bee are my eyes, you understand, they tell me what people look like, they keep tabs on all the suspects, and they never forget a face."

"All right, I get that… but the path to the cottage is really too muddy for your chair, Darren. I propose we wait until the local police show up with an ambulance and a forensics team, *then* I can charter a few men to carry you to the cottage, wheelchair and all, and you can do your thing, and after that I propose we all go for lunch in Dorking, after which I'll come back here to get on with my job, and you three can go home in the Suzuki, either back to London or on to Bottomleigh."

"Excellent plan, Collins," Daisy said, "but first you must help me put Darren into his chair while we wait for the reinforcements to arrive."

So that's what they did. Daisy and Collins transferred the paraplegic to his wheelchair, which they'd set up on a dry patch next to the drive, and sure enough, by the time they were done a caravan of police vehicles and an ambulance showed up on the forest track. Collins had to make sure that the newcomers didn't interfere with the tyre marks he'd spotted on the drive—Tyler's car was nowhere to be seen—and then he explained to them that he needed a few men to carry a paraplegic to the crime scene. Darren was hoisted from the ground by a couple of sturdy 'uniforms', who trudged with him along the muddy, overgrown trail from the cars to the cottage over a distance of about fifty yards. Daisy and Collins followed closely, and even Beatrice tagged along, ruining a pair of expensive shoes. When they'd deposited him inside the French windows, Darren rolled over towards the dead body slumped on the couch, took a good look, and then turned his head up to the police officer standing by his side.

"You know something, Detective Inspector? It's a good job that you went along with what we asked, because I know this man too. This is one of the two missing people we've been looking for all along, actually. This is not only Kevin Tyler, you understand, I happen to know him as well by the name of *Jack Reaper.*"

IV Too many paths the same way lead astray

When they were having lunch in Dorking, sitting in a quiet corner of a local pub, Daisy and Collins discussed the case at length, with Darren and Beatrice in attendance, and they all agreed that if Kevin Tyler, or Jack Reaper, had really been murdered the night before, then Greg Milton, also known as Lee Quincy, was their prime suspect.

"Are you sure about the *rigor mortis?*" Daisy asked her old acquaintance from the Yard, "and that the victim died only last night?"

"I have some experience with stiffs, you know, and the police surgeon seemed to agree with me when he arrived on the scene. But we'll know more when he delivers his report."

"It's true that you were always quite good with corpses, including the two that my Jonathan produced at the time... but in this case the only problem is that there's not a shred of evidence against Quincy so far."

"We will analyse those tyre tracks first thing," Collins assured them, "but even if he was stupid enough to leave his own car's traces on the crime scene, it still won't prove much,

I'm afraid."

"Oh, I agree. This is when the suspect guiltily stammers that he was there all right, but that the victim was already lying dead on the ground when he arrived."

"Exactly. We'll need more... Wait and see."

"But at least the man had motive and opportunity in a big way."

Just imagine what a shock it must have been, Daisy told them, when both men, their suspect and the victim, arrived at the Manor Hotel on the first day of the Murder Convention. They must have recognized each other the moment they set eyes on one another. They probably didn't let on that they'd ever met before, but Greg Milton in particular must have felt a burning urge to take revenge on the man who'd put him behind bars. The plot of 'Tables Turned in Hell', which Thea Slayer had already discussed with him, must only have confirmed his own suspicions, which he'd confided to Jonathan when he was still in jail, that Tyler was not just the detective who'd busted him, but possibly the man who'd staged the whole kidnapping, pocketed the ransom, and framed him for it.

"It makes you wonder if it could really have been a mere coincidence," Daisy concluded, "them both showing up at the convention like that."

"Only Milton himself will be able to tell us, at a later stage," Collins answered, "but we won't even be mentioning his name in our report, as long as we have no evidence of his presence on the scene," and he added, "At any rate I must ask the three of you to refrain from any further enquiries, especially you, Mrs Hayes. Leave this to the police, yes? We're on the case now."

"You're a good one to tell us off," Daisy grumbled, "without us no one would have found that body at least until next spring, and you might never have discovered its double identity."

"It seems ungrateful, I know, but I must insist. And what's more, I can't even mention your role in my report, I hope you don't mind."

Daisy smiled. "I can imagine why it would be a problem, and don't worry, I still appreciate the trouble you went through on account of us."

"And when you good people get back home," Collins said with a cautionary finger raised, that only Darren and Beatrice could see, "be careful not to show Quincy that you know who he really is."

"Of course! We'll keep our cards close to our chests."

But on their drive back to Bottomleigh Daisy was already planning her next move. She needed to find out if Quincy was still there, and if he might have left the premises the night before. Obviously she couldn't just ask him, or even interrogate the other writers in his presence, but that didn't matter. She could inquire discreetly about Quincy's movements from the staff, starting with Sondra, then sounding out the woman who'd last done his room, and ending with Mister Kumar when he would show up for duty that night. Surely he was no longer dozing off on the job these days. Another thing that absolutely needed to be looked into was Jack Reaper's literary career. Who was his publisher? How had the crack detective from the Bowen case ended up as a best-selling mystery writer under another name? So many interesting things to find out!

What's more, when they entered the hotel's lobby it became clear at once that they wouldn't need to make any efforts, particularly, to continue their investigation. Half a dozen mystery writers congregated around the new arrivals at once, as if they'd been lying in wait, scrutinizing the surroundings from behind the curtains, listening for the puttering of a Suzuki on the drive. They were eager to sound out the strange couple from the attic who'd been gone for more than twenty-four hours now, and started badgering them all at once. "My dear Daisy, Darren, where have you been? — Jack and Thea are still missing, you know! — We're all worried sick; something terrible must have happened. — Did you find out anything? Any news at all from your side?"

Daisy didn't have the heart not to disclose that Jack Reaper had been found dead by a detective from Scotland Yard she knew.

"And Thea?" they cried after a while, after they'd let the shocking news sink in, "did you hear anything about our dear Thea?"

"No, I'm awfully sorry, even the Metropolitan CID are still groping in the dark on that, but we have to expect the worst."

"But does this mean that *she* killed Jack? — And how do you know all this? — What have you been up to? — Please tell us all!"

Daisy had to disappoint her eager audience by announcing that she couldn't disclose any further details, that she'd already overstepped the orders from the police by revealing Jack Reaper's death.

"We have to wait; there's nothing more we can do for the moment; the Met have put their best people on it and are giving it the highest priority."

Meanwhile she had pricked up her ears and recognized Lee Quincy's voice within the group surrounding them, expressing the same concerns as the others, just as anxious as everybody else by the sound of it. If he was guilty, then he had to be a pretty good actor as well, she concluded, but that was only to be expected.

Darren now took his leave and proceeded to the elevator on his own, while Daisy introduced Beatrice to the group, if only to take their minds off the dramatic news she'd just imparted. The fact that Bee was the daughter of a marquess, of

112

a well-known Peer of the realm—not merely a dowager but the heiress in person—didn't fail to make a big impression. After which the two ladies, who were well attuned to each other and to working as a team, manoeuvred the whole group into the day lounge. "Let's all have a nice cuppa, or something stronger for those who need it."

Daisy wanted to get some more information out of the writers without appearing to be prying, the first question being: were all the participants still present, and what had they been up to? It soon transpired that only two people had disregarded DCI Gilford's instructions and gone home the day before: James Adam, the bumbling detective, and Jessica Holmes, the cupcake and cat lover had decided to call it a day. At least not at the top of the list of suspects, those two, Daisy concluded. The rest of the participants, precisely half a dozen, had stayed put and tried to make the best of a bad situation, spending many hours during the last two days reading mysteries, exchanging the books they'd taken along among themselves, and some of them even working on their current publishing projects. But they all felt bored and frustrated, and wondered obsessively where it would all end. "It's driving us up the wall," someone concluded.

"And I guess you've been going out a lot, to take your minds off things; roaming the countryside in your cars, I take it?"

Well, certainly, they all concurred, but even that went only so far, especially in this rainy weather. "Some of us have become quite devoted to The Fly and Fish," the sophisticated-sounding Ruth Vine gently mocked.

"Oh, by the way," Daisy said, "can anyone tell me the name of Jack's publisher? I'm sure the Met people will be looking into that as well, but I'm just curious."

"Jack and I have the same publisher," the elegant-sounding Jim Cross answered, "that is to say, we *had*... although

113

I suppose they still *are* his publishers even now... Scribblers & Sons, from London. They also publish Aggie's work."

"Yeah, Jim and I are colleagues, to my great sorrow," the youngest member of the club tittered girlishly.

So this would be the next step in her own investigation, Daisy concluded: getting Scribblers & Sons on the line and trying to find out more about how Kevin Tyler had become a best-selling author. Time to break up the charming reunion as soon as it was decently acceptable to do so. On their way to the flat a moment later she greeted Sondra, introduced her friend once more, and asked the friendly receptionist to look up the publisher's phone number on the computer, which she did at once with a short burst of ticking on her keyboard.

"Why don't you come up at the end of your shift?" Daisy told her, "I'll fill you in on the latest developments, and you can inform us about the situation here."

Then they walked on, Beatrice leading Daisy by the hand, quite unnecessarily, but before they could reach the elevator they were intercepted by Mister Robbins. He knew the lady friend well from previous visits, and was fully aware of her elevated social standing, which he clearly understood to be more genuine than that of his hotel's 'permanent resident'. This always led him to tedious, obsequious exchanges, like thanking Her Ladyship for "gracing his modest establishment with her presence". However, he could never refrain from hinting at the fact that a lady of her standing would surely be more comfortable as a 'regular, fully-fledged' guest of the Manor Hotel.

"Especially now," he remarked on this occasion, "as our humble inn has many regrettable vacancies."

But Daisy would have none of this; she drew the line at her inalienable right to put up as many of her friends for as long as she wanted in her own home. And if this... horrible little man imagined that poor Bee had any funds to spare on his overpriced rooms, he was sorely deluding himself.

"Your vacancies are neither here nor there, Robbins," she firmly asserted before she dragged her old friend into the lift.

Finally they joined Darren in the attic flat, and it felt as if the two of them had been gone for ages, while they'd only spent one night in London. "Now we'll have to move the massage table out of the guestroom, and it'll be all yours, darling Bee, for as long as you care to stay," Daisy said. But first that phone call needed to be made, before the end of the office hours came about. Beatrice told them what she knew about Scribblers & Sons: it was a big and successful company, focused on producing best-sellers, "But they're a bit of an upstart in the publishing business, they don't have the tradition and the *class* of Alexander and Custer, therefore I don't know anyone who works for them. I'm afraid I can't help you there."

Daisy picked up the phone regardless, hoping she could winkle whoever answered it into putting her through to Jack Reaper's editor. But no such luck. This time she hit a snag, in the form of a snooty switchboard girl who told her haughtily that if she wasn't able to tell her his name, she probably didn't have any business talking to him.

"This is a serious company, we can't let the general public just barge in on us, you understand."

"Yes, but I have some important information for Jack Reaper's editor, as it happens."

"Are you an unpublished author by any chance? Pestering leading editors will get you nowhere, I can assure you."

When Daisy slammed down the receiver, Beatrice tutted and advised her not to take it out on the poor 'blower', "Everything went so smoothly until now, you were bound to be stymied sooner or later."

"Yes, but why must I be defeated by a lowly switchboard

operator in the end?"

Then Darren reminded them that they should move the massage table now, and allow dear Beatrice to take her things to her room. "Welcome to Bottomleigh House, anyway."

It took some time before Daisy could finally talk to Mister Kumar and gather some interesting information about Lee Quincy's movements. First she'd sounded out Sondra, when she came by at the end of her shift, but the receptionist's report on the activities of the convention's participants didn't add much to the picture provided by the writers themselves earlier on. They'd been hanging around, keeping themselves busy with novels and manuscripts, had gone for walks and drives into the countryside, but there was nothing suspect to report about any individual in particular.

Then Daisy, Darren and Beatrice had gone down to the restaurant for dinner with the company, after which some postprandial drinks and exchanges of gossip hadn't brought any new information to light either. Especially as they needed to put on an uninterested demeanour so as not to draw Lee Quincy's attention on their interest in him. But finally, when all the guests had retired to their rooms and Darren and Beatrice had been sent up to the flat, Daisy had Kumar to herself and could sound him out again.

"Mister Quincy did go out last night and didn't come back until the small hours. I heard his car drive up at around two in the morning."

"Really? Now that's interesting..."

"...But that's nothing new: he's been going to The Fish and Fly every night since the beginning of the convention. He told me the other night that he'd spotted the place on the Horsham road on the day he arrived here, and has been a regular since then."

"Oh. I suppose that's what Mrs Vine meant when she said that some had become quite devoted to the place."

"True, I believe she even accompanied him there at least once. And don't forget that this infamous pub provided Mr Quincy with an excellent alibi on the night of the scream. He's been boasting ever since that he's the only guest who has one."

"Ah, yes, Mr Wilson, his publisher, told me the same thing. He even called it 'an ironclad alibi'... Well, thank you, Mister Kumar, you've been most helpful."

While she went up to the loft flat Daisy reflected that Kumar's testimony was not directly damning for Quincy, exactly, but didn't exonerate him either, far from it. Even if several witnesses had spotted him at The Fly and Fish at different moments the night before, he could still have slipped away and driven over to Dorking and back between revels. In the end all would depend on the results of the tyre tread investigation.

Then, when she reported her findings to the two others, Darren made a rather satirical remark about The Fly and Fish being DS Mundie's favourite haunt as well. "Maybe the sarge himself saw Quincy there last night! Wouldn't that put a damper on your hopes for nailing him?"

"Very funny, honeybunch."

But that's when she suddenly remembered the remark DC Hardy had made to his superior on the first night, when the police had come to investigate 'the scream': "Sarge, remember what you said? That I shouldn't tell anyone *where* I picked you up tonight?"

In the light of recent developments those words took on a new meaning, and Daisy decided she would have to get DC Hardy on the phone first thing in the morning. At least the switchboard operator at the West Sussex CID knew her and wouldn't have any objections to putting her through. But for now it was time to go to bed and get some sleep, well deserved after a long and eventful day.

— 2 —

So Theodora Slayer had killed Jack Reaper after all, DCI Gilford reflected, and not the other way round. Incredible! You didn't expect such a thing from a woman. But then again... the victim had been attacked from behind, apparently, garrotted with some thin cord that left a deep mark around his neck. What a sneaky and vicious way of killing someone, typical of a female perpetrator: the poor man never saw it coming.

Sitting in his glass cubicle the next morning, he was going through the paperwork that had just arrived from London, that is to say, the 'computer printout' of a report drawn up by a certain DI Collins from the Met. Never heard of him.

The gall of some people; that man had called in an intervention team from Surrey Division, including forensics and a police surgeon, and then New Scotland Yard had claimed the credit for finding the dead body. What on earth had this detective from London been *doing* in the middle of nowhere, in the Surrey Hills of all places, and what business did he have making that find? Did he just stumble on a corpse while looking for a nice spot for a picnic? It made you wonder.

On the other hand, the mystery could be explained quite simply by the fact that Jack Reaper had been identified by "several witnesses" as none other than Kevin Tyler, *another* Scotland Yard detective, this one quite famous. So maybe DI Collins had just been looking for his colleague in an entirely different affair. But in that case you had to ask yourself: what was the relationship between the two cases? Between 'the hut in the woods' and 'the scream in the night'? Between

Kevin Tyler and Jack Reaper? These writers and their pseudonyms! Did they all have fake identities? It made your head spin!

Gilford sighed and looked over at his underlings sitting at their desks on the other side of the glass partition. They were still engrossed in their daily routine, meaning that they had little to do, except for writing important-looking reports about doing almost nothing. DC Hardy, not incidentally, seemed to be the only one who was actually doing some serious work, engaged in lengthy consultations on the phone, unless he was just talking to his missus... On the other hand, those of his colleagues who were staring the most intently at their computer screens were probably engrossed in some electronic version of a solitaire game of cards. Frowning at the ungainly sight, their chief reflected that now that a corpse had finally turned up, they at last had a case, and that was a positive development in its own right, very good news indeed. "High time to shake these worthless slackers out of their complacency," he told himself.

The thing is, he'd also just received instructions from the Division Commissioner to the effect that they, the West Sussex CID, should fully cooperate with the Met on the case. Their first task would be to compare a tyre pattern that had been found on the crime scene with those of all the writers' vehicles in the Manor Hotel's parking lot. And as his men hadn't collected any tyre marks yet (why should they have?) this meant they'd need to trundle over to Bottomleigh again and do so now.

Gilford sighed as he took a good look at the 'enhanced' photograph from the Surrey forensics team, also a printout from the computer. Enhanced or not, one tyre mark looked much like any other, he always thought, but obviously the proof would be in the comparison. Still, a pretty humdrum task. And that was another thing he found rather galling;

why should he take orders from London on this thing? There was no reason why the Met should be in charge of the investigation, all of a sudden. Those from Surrey had already contributed an important part of the paperwork: the death certificate, post-mortem, and official identification of the victim; all the forensic evidence collected on the scene, including that tyre pattern. They could have claimed the case for themselves for the simple reason that the stiff had turned up in Surrey... but instead they'd been reporting directly to London like a bunch of obedient little lambs... and meanwhile the Murder Convention, where it had all started, was still ongoing in West Sussex! So there.

"High time to seize back the initiative and take the lead in this matter," DCI Gilford reflected.

Unfortunately, that was easier said than done. He started racking his brains, gabling his fingers in front of his lips, and wondered how, exactly, one could go about showing up those know-it-alls from the Met.

Then he suddenly remembered the paper snippet.

What on earth had happened to it? He couldn't remember pocketing it or slipping it into his wallet, let alone filing it away at the office, so he must have left it behind at the Manor Hotel, he concluded. It had slipped his mind completely until now. While Mrs Hayes had so contritely owned up to taking it from the fireplace on the crime scene, and Mr Miller had so dutifully relinquished it in his hands, he had neglected to pay any attention to it at all. How remiss on his part! But it had to be in their possession still; hopefully the couple hadn't thrown it away. Gilford was overtaken by an irresistible urge to go over to their place at once and speak to Mrs Hayes. Whether the paper snippet was still there or not, she would be able to tell him more about its significance... Wouldn't it be wonderful if it turned out to be an important clue after all, giving the West Sussex CID a providential leg-up on those snooty little prats from the Met?

Time for action.

The chief stood up abruptly, full of hope and renewed energy, and stepping out of his glass cubicle into the main office space, he stood there, smirking, as all his underlings interrupted whatever they were doing on their computers and waited for what was to come.

"You... you... and you: two cars. We're off to Bottomleigh. We have some important work to do."

When they turned up on the gravel drive in front of the hotel, the delegation from the West Sussex CID made an impression almost as overwhelming as the first time they'd come out in force. That's why the Chief had ordered two cars, although they were with only four people: the Chief himself, the sarge and the constable, plus a uniformed 'Sherpa' to drive the Chief and carry his briefcase. They would have easily fitted in one car, but would have made only half the impression. They stormed the lobby all the same, made a beeline for reception and demanded to see the manager. When the Chief had stated his business to Mister Robbins, flashing his badge at him, his three underlings went out to the parking lot, and he ordered the receptionist to "call Mrs Hayes and ask her to activate the lift for me." Then he disappeared as by magic behind the sliding steel doors, while Sondra, at her desk, shook her head and tutted.

First DCI Gilford was slightly taken aback by Beatrice's presence in the loft flat; he hadn't counted on a visitor; the presence of the wheelchair-bound husband was irritating enough as a rule. At least the lady in question greeted him most graciously, and was introduced as a marchioness, which was not to be sneezed at. But then Daisy had to disappoint her guest cruelly, when he asked about the snippet.

"I'm afraid I no longer have it, Inspector, but I didn't

discard it, have no fear. It is now in the possession of a detective from Scotland Yard, DI Collins, you may have heard of him."

"Yes, I was reading his report only this morning. If he kept it, this piece of evidence must have been important after all, but you should have given it to *me*, Mrs Hayes."

"Well, you seemed to have mislaid it, so I thought I could set things right by giving it to Collins, who's an old acquaintance."

So that's how those snooty little prats from the Met have gotten onto the case, Gilford reflected despondently.

"Be that as it may," he intoned, "we, of the West Sussex CID, are now in the process of wrapping up the case, Madam. As we speak my men are checking the tyres of all the cars in the lot, comparing them to the tread marks found on the murder scene. I'm pretty sure they will find a match with Mrs Slayer's old Bentley, which is still there, I spotted it when we arrived."

"She had a Bentley too?" Beatrice sighed nostalgically, "how quaint!"

"But Inspector," Daisy exclaimed, "surely you're not thinking that it's *Thea Slayer* who murdered Jack Reaper? And why would she have brought her car back, where is she hiding now?"

"All in good time, Mrs Hayes, the investigation is still ongoing."

"Yes, but you *do* realize that Reaper was killed only the night before last, and therefore his death probably has nothing to do with 'the night of the scream' and Thea's disappearance. I'm afraid she's dead too, but we still have to find her body."

"Really, do you reckon?"

This time DCI Gilford was much taken aback, the lady seemed to have a valid point. And if she was right, there had to be a *third* person involved, who'd murdered Mrs Slayer *and* Mr Reaper both. Daisy, meanwhile, was reflecting that this was a golden opportunity to find out more about the relationship between Kevin Tyler and Greg Milton. In particular, by what coincidence had the two ended up at the Murder Convention? Or had it been by design? And if so, *whose* design?

"Excuse me, Inspector... If you read Collins's report, then you know that Jack Reaper's real name was Kevin Tyler, whom you've surely heard about in connection with the famous Bowen case. Now, only yesterday afternoon I was trying to find out more about the man, I called his publishers in London, but they flatly turned me down."

The chief perked up. "Does Collins know about this?"

"No, he doesn't, although he might help me too, but I'm asking *you*. Could you phone them and throw around your weight a bit? I'd like you to ask them, first, if they know the real identity of their star author, and secondly, how did he become a best-selling mystery writer?"

"All right, give me their number."

What happened next was quite wonderful to witness: the chief inspector seemed to relish the opportunity to take charge and put that snooty switchboard girl in her place, and although they only heard their own end of the conversation, they enjoyed it very much. Darren silently rolled over to his wife and squeezed her hand, exchanging amused glances with Beatrice.

You had stern authority: "Yes... Detective Chief Inspector Marc Gilford, of the West Sussex CID speaking. Could you get me Mr Jack Reaper's editor on the line, please? Thank you."

You had veiled threats: "Yes, well, if you don't want to take my word for it I can fax a summons, and your superior will be required to report *in person* to our precinct in Horsham,

West Sussex, before the end of the day, so why don't you let *him* decide for himself what he prefers?"

You had wounded pride: "This is a *murder* investigation, my dear girl, so I have *every* right to 'just barge in like that', believe you me!"

You had mock cajoling: "Ah, Mr Fisher, at last! I was just thinking: if the mountain won't come to Muhammad, and all that..."

Finally you had token sympathy and no-nonsense urgency: "Yes, bad news I'm afraid... Mr Reaper was found dead, this is now a murder investigation... are you aware of your author's *real* identity?"

Then they couldn't catch much, apart from "I see... yes... you don't say," at regular intervals. But after putting down the phone the Chief could tell them *exactly* how matters stood. He reported proudly that when Kevin Tyler had been at the height of his fame as a hero detective, he'd received many offers from various publishers to make a book from his story. But according to Mr Fisher, the editor, when the famous man had accepted his offer, he set the condition that he would write under a pseudonym, first of all, and that he would launch into a series of detective novels based on his experience. "I know the ropes," he'd proudly asserted, "and I don't want to thank my success to my celebrity." It had sounded very noble indeed, the editor remarked, and in due course the books became a huge success. Everybody satisfied.

"Extraordinary!" Daisy exclaimed, "so it *could* have been a coincidence after all."

"What's that, my dear?" Gilford asked, pricking up his ears.

"Well, you see, Thea was working on the Bowen case too. She was writing a novel about it. That's what we learned in London from the snippet we found in the hearth. But... she may not have been aware of the fact that Jack Reaper was *the* famous detective... he was invited for the first time... and she may not have paid much attention to the photos of him that appeared in the press and on television fifteen years ago. Yes, it could well be that his presence here was a pure coincidence."

"But what does it *mean?* Please tell me!"

Now Daisy was in something of a quandary. Should she mention Lee Quincy, and reveal what she knew about him? After all, Collins had admonished her to leave it alone, and to let *him* and his colleagues from the Met deal with it. But poor Gilford was so visibly eager to make his mark in this investigation, that she decided to confide in him out of pure kind-heartedness.

"It means that the Bowen case is the key to this whole affair. Are you familiar with it? Does the name Greg Milton ring a bell?"

"I remember the affair only vaguely... as for Greg Milton, it sounds familiar, somehow, but I couldn't say exactly where from."

"He was also involved at the time, and it's Lee Quincy's real name."

"Really? We did do some pretty thorough background checks on all those writers, you know, but their true identities are a well-kept secret. The only alias we were able to unravel was Mrs Slayer's: her real name is Dorothy Vine."

"Yes, interesting, but Greg Milton is the man who was put away by Kevin Tyler, and he has become a person of interest since the man who nabbed him was found dead."

"Ah, I see. So you think we should arrest him, or at least interrogate him under caution?"

"No. For the moment there is absolutely no evidence placing him at the crime scene, unless that tyre pattern turns out to be his car's"

"You think that will be the case? I still expect it will turn out to be Mrs Slayer's Bentley."

"Yes, well, but even if there's no match, I've just realised that Mr Milton is a key witness of what happened in the night of the scream, even though the two affairs are probably not even related. You know about his 'ironclad alibi'?"

"Yes, naturally! I'm still leading that part of the investigation, you know."

"Quite so. But has it occurred to you that Milton, or Quincy, could have *seen* something when he drove back to the hotel from The Fly and Fish on that night? Admittedly he was quite inebriated, but he must have passed Reaper's Jaguar driving in the opposite direction, heading for Dorking and the Surrey Hills."

"And what if he did?"

"It would be interesting to *gauge* his reaction if we interrogate him about it. Just an 'innocuous interview', mind you, in order to dot the i's and cross the t's, supposedly. Could you do that for me?"

"If you ask so nicely, I find it hard to say no. But I must confess that my head is spinning, rather, with all these awfully complicated theories you seem to be churning out constantly in that clever head of yours."

Darren now piped up: "I tend to agree with you, Chief Inspector, I kind of feel the same."

"Me too," Beatrice concurred.

"Well I'm only trying to be helpful," Daisy grumbled, "and besides, this may be worth it, my dear Inspector, because I'm pretty sure DI Collins and his colleagues haven't thought of it... for the time being."

"Very well, then let's talk to the man!"

But right then they were interrupted by the phone ringing on the coffee table. It was Sondra, calling from reception to say that Detective Sergeant Mundie needed to speak to his boss urgently, and demanded to be sent up with the lift. Moments later the elevator's doors slid open and he irrupted into the lofty room where the four of them were sitting around the coffee table.

"Governor! We found a match! You're not going to believe this, but that tyre pattern they sent us is exactly the same as on Theodora Slayer's Bentley!"

"That's what I expected all along," the Chief remarked smugly, "I knew it! Mrs Hayes, didn't I say so from the start?"

— 3 —

When Daisy had talked to Hardy on the phone earlier that morning, the poor constable had had little choice but to confirm her suspicions. And what's more, he had to do it in veiled terms because the culprit was sitting at a desk quite close to his own in the open office space of the Horsham CID.

"Yes, I remember those words, Madam… you're right, I was referring to the establishment you just mentioned, the gentleman in question spent the whole evening there, but I was sworn to secrecy about… what happened. So I must ask you urgently to respect that, if you see what I mean."

Daisy had smiled at the one-sided hush-hush character of this conversation, but she couldn't help pointing out the potential problems that could arise from this situation.

"I won't rat on the sergeant, don't you worry my dear Constable, but you must admit that there's now a disturbing possibility for the suspect to *blackmail* him. What if Mr Quincy asks Mundie to provide him with a false alibi for the night Jack Reaper was murdered? You see what I mean? *'You must tell them I was at the pub with you at that moment, then I won't tell anyone what you were up to that other time.'* Do you know if the sarge was on duty, the night before last?"

No, he had not been on duty, Hardy told her, and he *could* have spent a couple of hours at the said establishment.

So Daisy still needed Gilford to interview Quincy for her, but she'd better not tell him exactly why. Just an innocuous interview in order to dot the i's and cross the t's. However, for now the Chief was completely in thrall to the news about the tyre pattern of Thea's Bentley. So first she *also* needed to explain to him, diplomatically, mind you, that the matching treads didn't mean that *she*, Thea, had murdered Reaper in the Surrey woods, *necessarily*.

"Do you remember the unknown person who entered the building through the basement window, Inspector? We concluded that the suspect must have received some help from outside, and that if these confederates had murdered Thea, they could have gotten hold of her car keys quite easily."

"So you're suggesting that there might be a *third* person involved after all, who murdered Mrs Slayer *and* Mr Reaper both?"

"Yes, something like that, and what's more, it *might* be one of the writers. What if this accomplice didn't enter the building *before* the crime, like we assumed, but instead returned inside through the cellar window *after* helping to carry the body to Reaper's car, and *then* joined the others?"

"I prefer to assume that it's Mrs Slayer who killed Mr Reaper, that's much more likely."

"All right, but how about interviewing Quincy all the same? I'm still interested in what he'll have to say for himself."

Moments later they were finally talking to the man Daisy still saw as their prime suspect, in a quiet corner of the day lounge, just Gilford and her. Darren and Beatrice had joined the others for a nice cuppa in the library, which had been made available again by the police. First the inspector went over Quincy's alibi on the night of the scream once more, at

Daisy's suggestion, and as expected, the Chief seemed to assume that several members of the public had seen him in The Fly and Fish that night, and had testified to that effect. While he repeated his own story, Quincy didn't mention at all that he'd spotted Mundie there as well. Exactly as could be expected, Daisy thought.

"Now, if I may put my oar in a bit, Inspector, may I ask our friend here if he saw anything interesting on the road, afterwards? Think back carefully, my dear Quincy, you were a bit tipsy, but do you remember seeing any other vehicles on your way back to the hotel?"

"Well, yes, I did actually, but only in a flash of my headlights, as the Horsham road is not lighted at night between agglomerations. I thought that I crossed Reaper's Jaguar, with Thea sitting next to him in the passenger seat, but I didn't pay much attention to it at the time..."

"Could you see if Mrs slayer was still alive?" DCI Gilford asked eagerly, "was she wounded, or did she seem all right?"

"That I can't say with certainty, sir. She could have been alive, but when I arrived at the hotel and heard what had happened, I just assumed she must have been dead when I caught a glimpse of her."

"So no definitive verdict there, how frustrating! And why didn't you mention any of this in your testimony?"

"No one asked, and besides, like you say, I wasn't positive about what I did or didn't see, so I thought it wiser to let it rest."

Daisy reflected that Quincy, or Greg Milton, must at least have had a pretty fair idea where his nemesis was headed. And when he'd heard that a crime had been committed and that the corpse and the killer had disappeared, there would have been no doubt in his mind that Kevin Tyler would drive straight to 'the hut in the woods' near Dorking.

"And how about the night before last?" she now asked.

"You mean the night Jack Reaper was killed? What about it?"

"Do you have an alibi for that night as well? I know you haven't been asked yet; no one has been interviewed by the police, I guess, but I'm just wondering."

"Well, as it happens I spent the evening at The Fly and Fish again, and your own Sergeant Mundie can vouch for it, Inspector. He was there as well."

"Well that's capital!" Gilford exclaimed, "If we can confirm your alibi that easily, then you're completely off the hook, in the clear, as clean as a whistle!"

He sounded a bit too enthusiastic, Daisy thought, and she knew all too well why that was.

"You don't seem entirely convinced, my dear Daisy," Quincy remarked, "I can see a doubtful frown on your brow."

"I was just reflecting how convenient this alibi provided by a police officer is for you. Once again you'll probably turn out to be the only person around who has one."

"Well, no, I was coming to that. Do you remember the conversations that took place in the lobby, and later in the day lounge, when you came back yesterday afternoon? When our dear Ruth, Ruth Vine, said that some of us have become quite devoted to The Fly and Fish? Well in fact she was referring to the night before. I took her there, so she has an alibi too. We drove over in my car, and stayed together until the small hours, sampling the local bitter and talking about sweet nothings like a pair of lovelorn teenagers."

"There you are then!" DCI Gilford exclaimed with undisguised relish.

— 4 —

Daisy was now in a double quandary. Should she get in touch with Collins about the latest developments? It looked

130

like their main suspect was off the hook, as Gilford had pointed out all too eagerly. But hadn't Daisy promised to refrain from any further enquiries, hadn't she been told to leave it to the police? And what's more, Collins would be receiving reports from the West Sussex CID soon enough, and could draw his own conclusions about Thea's Bentley. Daisy had *told* him about the accomplice who'd entered through the basement window.

On the other hand, how could she get Gilford to focus on the real issue, finding Thea's dead body? Daisy didn't doubt for one moment that she must have been dead when Quincy spotted her in the passenger seat of Reaper's Jaguar. Yet the Chief was still bent on arresting her for murder. He'd ordered the Bentley to be 'turned inside out' by his habitual forensic team, and apparently he intended to wait for their results without doing anything further. The investigation would be on hold for a while yet.

"What do you hope to achieve?" she asked him as he paced the lobby while he waited for the 'experts' to arrive, "I can tell you already now that you'll find plenty of Thea's fingerprints everywhere in that car!"

"Yes," he answered tetchily, stopping in his tracks for brief moment, "but we'll *also* be looking for traces from the crime scene in the woods, you know."

"Well, we already know that the *car* was there, but the real question you should be investigating now, is *where* is Mrs Slayer? Never mind whether she's dead or alive."

"Yes, yes, I know all that… all in due course, Mrs Hayes, please don't tell me how to do my job and just let me get on with it, won't you?"

"No, I'm afraid I must insist, and pester you some more. Can't you and your team do *both things* at the same time? If you want to upstage DI Collins and his colleagues from the Met, that's what you should be doing, you should be seen to *anticipate* the next steps of the investigation, regardless of the outcome."

"What on earth does that even *mean?*"

"Do you have detailed maps at your precinct? I bet you have... you know: *maps*, of Southern England and such, covering the region, including Surrey maybe."

"Supposing we have, what do you want me to do with them?"

"You could check the *route* Mr Reaper and Mrs Slayer followed that night. Quincy's testimony tells us they were driving due north, we may safely assume they were heading for the hut in the woods, so where, along the way, could Mr Reaper have dropped Mrs Slayer off, dead or alive? A careful scrutiny of a detailed set of maps could enlighten us about that, you see what I mean? And if we do it right now, we *might* find something interesting before the others do."

That last remark did the trick, as Daisy had hoped it would. She knew quite well which buttons to push by now.

"All right, let's go and have a look at our maps... but I want you to come along... maybe you can give me some feedback in the process."

"With great pleasure!"

That is how Daisy and Gilford ended up in his partitioned-off private office at the CID headquarters in Horsham, pouring over maps on his desk—at least the inspector poured, bending over them, peering intently at the roads leading from Bottomleigh to Dorking and beyond. Darren and Beatrice had been left behind to amuse themselves on their own at the Manor Hotel.

"Now what should I be looking for, according to you?" Gilford asked, genuinely puzzled.

"Well, let's just assume for one moment that Thea is dead and that Reaper needed to dispose of her body. It's not your favourite hypothesis, I know, but the nice thing about a hypothesis is that it can easily be verified. You can think up a pretty complex scenario without actually having a shred of evidence to support it, and *then* check if it's true or not."

"You make it sound so easy, my dear."

"But it is, in a way! All I'm asking is that you disprove my theory if you can, so you may exclude it from your investigation from now on. This will only take a few hours."

"And what would that theory be?"

Gilford sounded amused rather than annoyed, so Daisy felt encouraged to pursue her advantage.

"Well here it is: listen to my line of reasoning. I first assumed that our killer must have dumped the body in the *pond* on the hotel grounds, remember? Now we know for a fact that he drove away with it. But he *must* have considered the pond as a *possibility* when he was setting off, right? So he *could* have dropped the body *in another pond*, at the most convenient location on his way to the hut in the woods. And which location would that be? Well, as close as possible to the hut, so he could easily abandon the car by the pond—or ditch it in the water too—and walk on to his hiding place. Let's not forget that his Jag hasn't been found either."

Therefore what 'they' should be looking for on the maps, Daisy concluded, were ponds or small lakes close enough to the hut and to the roads, so that Jack Reaper, or Kevin Tyler, might have known of their existence from his earlier dealings with that location. "He had to be able to find them in the middle of the night."

She heard the rustling of maps being smoothed down on the desk in front of her, and Gilford muttered, "Now let's see," clearly taken in by the challenge. It didn't require much time before he could conclude that there were at least *three* ponds on locations that corresponded to the parameters set out by Daisy, and therefore fitted the bill.

"Only three?" she cried, "but that's perfect! If you send out a team of your brilliant bloodhounds in a car at once, they should be able to check them out within a few hours! They should be back with answers before the end of the day, this afternoon, even."

Yes, Gilford reflected, as he surveyed the main office space beyond the glass partition once again. He concluded that the remainder of his team, sitting there at their desks, could clearly do with an urgent and arduous task at that moment. "Very well, Mrs Hayes, I will brief my men and send them on their way at once."

"Good. And as soon as they're off, you may take me back to Bottomleigh, if that's all right with you. We'll have lunch with Darren and Beatrice, and afterwards, if you please, there's another hypothesis I would like to verify with your assistance."

"That sounds rather ominous, and intriguing at the same time, my dear lady."

After lunch they all repaired to the pond by the side of the hotel: Daisy, Gilford, Darren and Bee, as well as Mister Robbins and the head gardener of the establishment. First they surveyed the part of its shore closest to the parking lot, scrutinizing the depths of its murky waters—at least those who could scrutinize. But to no avail.

"It could be lying quite close to us," Daisy assured them, "don't you see any twinkling of silver at all?"

No, the others assured her, no trace of that big silver candlestick to be seen.

"In that case, Mr Deeprose, I suggest that you do what we've discussed... if it's not too much trouble."

"Not at all, Your Ladyship, it will only take about an hour."

The man was the grandson of a head gardener of bygone days, and he insisted on addressing the widow of his grandfather's Lord's son with the title she was due by rights. He started walking briskly around the pond, and the others, who had nothing better to do in the meantime, followed him, 'Her Ladyship' pushing her husband's wheelchair along the familiar gravel path. When they reached the other side of the water, the gardener turned around and drew their attention to the fact that they were now standing on a kind of dike, a man-made dam, "even if you'd never guess if you didn't know."

He pointed at a shallow ditch that passed through a wide pipe under the path, and at an inconspicuous jumble of metal girders and wooden planks, half-hidden in the undergrowth that proliferated a bit further off. "This is the sluice that regulates the water level in the pond," he announced with proprietary pride, "I will now open it to the max, and then, as I said, it will take about an hour for the mudflats by the parking lot to fall dry." Then he bent over the antiquated, half-rusted installations, huffed and rummaged somewhat, and they suddenly heard a mighty gurgling sound, although there wasn't much to be seen. Clearly the pond was now emptying itself into a lower-lying stream.

"It's easy enough!" Daisy exclaimed, "we should have done this long before now... So, back to the parking lot, and let's see what will emerge."

It didn't even take an hour. Mr Deeprose was the one who spotted the silver candlestick emerging from the murky waters. It had landed in the mud only a few feet from the side, but it was stuck deep into the mud, head first, in a manner of speaking, and its broad base was covered with a layer of dark-grey felt, that had been pasted on to prevent scratches on the marble mantelpiece. The head gardener was wearing wellingtons; he stepped right onto the pond's muddy bank to retrieve it.

"Careful not to leave any prints on it!" Gilford admonished

him.

"I'll put on my work gloves then, Guv'?" he mumbled, and moments later he was back on the path and waited for the Chief to put on a pair of rubber gloves too before taking the heavy object over from him with great care.

"Do you think one can still find fingerprints or usable blood traces on it, Inspector?" Daisy asked.

"I honestly have no idea, but as our forensics colleagues are busy with the Bentley right over there, I'll just go over and give it to them at once."

"What do you make of this, though?" Daisy insisted as they followed the Chief to the parking lot, "someone must have thrown it into the water from the car park, no? Do you reckon that the distance between the spot where Reaper's Jag was parked and the pond could have been bridged in this manner?"

"Yes, possibly, but that would have been a mighty throw, you know."

"Exactly, more likely by an athletic young man like Jack Reaper than by a mature lady like Theodora Slayer."

As Gilford handed the candlestick to his forensic experts, Daisy told them that it might be the murder weapon, that they should handle it with care and give it their best.

"You're really enjoying this, aren't you?" the inspector grumbled as they headed back to the hotel. Mister Robbins was still tagging along, but not the head gardener, who'd gone back to the 'dam' to close the sluice again.

"Listen, you have to admit this puts the whole affair in a different light. How likely is it that Thea Slayer hit Jack Reaper over the head with a heavy candlestick *and then threw it all the way into the pond?* And if she didn't, it must have been the other way round, and she would at least have been badly injured. So, if you still believe that 'Thea killed Reaper' is the simplest explanation, I can only say 'Think

136

again'. You'll have to come up with a pretty complicated story to keep it standing, don't you agree?"

Gilford said nothing, he only sighed, and led the whole procession back inside the hotel. Then he asked Daisy if they could talk, in private, and the two of them retreated to a quiet corner of the day lounge again, leaving the others to fend for themselves. Sitting cosily together on their favourite sofa they made a charming pair, Beatrice reflected as she wheeled Darren into the library for their afternoon cuppa.

"Now, Mrs Hayes, I'm feeling a bit confused," the inspector said, "one moment you're telling me that my idea that Mrs Slayer could be our killer is *absurd*, and then you start suggesting that the culprit *must* be Mr Quincy, who turns out to have a perfectly valid alibi... So which is it? What am I to make of all this? Where do we stand?"

Daisy put her hand on Gilford's arm and gave him a reassuring little squeeze. "My dear Inspector, I'll grant you that this is a rather complicated case, but the whole thing is becoming clearer and clearer in my mind as we progress... I admit that I was wrong about Quincy, it seems he's innocent after all. As for Thea, let's wait until we've heard from the search party you've sent up north. If they find her body, the police surgeon will be able to tell us when she died. And if she died in the 'night of the scream', we'll know for certain she didn't kill Jack Reaper."

"All right, but if that turns out to be the case, then who did?"

"That will be the next stage of our investigation. I think it must be a woman, and what's more, she must have a nice soprano voice... Actually, it's a pity that Jessica Holmes went home, she might be a suspect after all."

"A *woman*? And I was under the impression that you're dead set against the very notion!" the inspector grumbled reproachfully.

V The truth can be a gift and a betrayal in one

— 1 —

The next day was Daisy's birthday. Darren and Beatrice congratulated her at the breakfast table, but they didn't have any presents for her and didn't expect any kind of party or celebration. Daisy always said that past the age of sixty, birthdays lost their use and their appeal, the least said the better and all that. She didn't want anyone to go to any trouble about it, and certainly didn't want them to buy her useless gifts. But on that morning she suddenly announced that she wished to offer them a treat, downstairs, the two of them, the staff, and the half-dozen guests who were still staying at the hotel. "Even Robbins will be welcome to join us today." It should be a cosy little party with all the trimmings, including a big round cake with candles, and the singing of a couple of classic birthday ditties. "But still no presents, as it's a bit too short notice for that."

She reflected wistfully that getting some news from Gilford about the search for Thea's body would have been the nicest birthday present of all, but the Chief had this quirky habit of going all formal at the most inconvenient moment, suddenly announcing in a huff that he couldn't share any information about an ongoing police investigation with members of the public, "if you don't mind." Just when you thought you'd managed to tame the man, to domesticate him somewhat.

After breakfast they went down, and while Darren and Beatrice went off to have a look at the daily papers, Daisy enlisted Sondra's help to organize her party. First a big, long hug from the receptionist, then finding the number of a well-known local bakery and ordering a big round cake to be delivered before coffee time—including a few candles if possible. And while Sondra went off to inform the staff members and organize some plates and cutlery, Daisy joined the others at the reading table. "Any news from the police yet?"

"No, nothing, precious. But don't you worry, when they go public about the case, the headlines will be screaming all over the front pages!"

"True. Now, Bee, about that little party, I need your help."

First, Beatrice would have to be the one who launched the whole company into a couple of spirited singalongs. 'Happy Birthday to You' and 'For She's a Jolly Good Fellow' would do nicely for a start. "But then I'll need your eyes and ears, and yours too, Darren, but Bee is the one who goes to the opera and all that." Beatrice would have to identify anyone who sang along in a *natural soprano voice*, make sure to distinguish which woman, or *women*, did this within the group present, in such a way that she might testify about it in a court of law if necessary. "But discreetly, mind you, we don't want to give the game away."

"But I don't *know* everybody," Beatrice protested, "I haven't been introduced to the members of the staff, for one thing."

"You don't need to identify anyone by name, at first: being

able to point out who has a soprano voice would be good enough. Then Darren can tell us who they are. Me, I can only listen, but even so I may be able to corroborate your and Darren's findings."

"What an extraordinary assignment! Why on earth are you looking for a *soprano?*"

"It's something Mister Kumar, the night porter, told me at the beginning about 'the scream', which Darren and I never heard, as you know. He said it came from a woman, and that she had 'a beautiful soprano voice'. At the time we all assumed that the scream came from the victim, but now I'm trying to find out if it could have been an accomplice: a *staged* scream, in other words."

"Interesting. The things you come up with!"

"Daisy's unwrapping her birthday present already," Darren sniggered.

At length, after the guests had finished their breakfast in the big dining room and had gone about their own business for a while, they started trickling into the library for their morning coffee, and Daisy's little party suddenly took off. The birthday cake with blazing candles was carried in by the kitchen hands, beaming as proudly as if they'd baked it themselves. Other staff was herded in by Sondra, carrying a few bottles of champagne and a hamper-full of flute glasses to serve it in. It had been Sondra's idea to charge some drinks to Jack Reaper's account, because his bill was not going to be settled in donkey's years anyway. They all congratulated the birthday girl, and hugged her, and made her blow the seven candles on the cake, one for every decade and the remainder tactfully ignored, before cutting it and handing it around. Finally, when they all had a glass of champagne Beatrice, with her long experience as a society hostess, brought out a toast, took one sip, and then led the whole company in a roaring rendition of Happy Birthday and Jolly Good Fellow.

Everybody joined in with heartfelt gusto: Tatyana, Agnieszka and Ilona; Kiyana, Jayden and Shanise, as well as the remaining mystery writers, they all sang along without an afterthought. A great success. A great success indeed.

The cheerful hubbub in the library eventually lured Robbins out of his quarters, and before he accepted a glass of bubbly in his turn he couldn't refrain from remarking that 'the attic residents' weren't supposed to use the hotel's premises for private celebrations, "at least not without asking my permission first."

"Oh, Robbins, must you always be such a party pooper?" Daisy chided him almost fondly, "Here, have a piece of cake, it's on me!"

And then, to top off an enjoyable celebration, the West Sussex CID raided the hotel once more, which was now in the process of becoming an almost daily occurrence. But this time it was Detective Constable Hardy who led a pack of uniformed men into the library. Without a word they made a beeline for Lee Quincy, apparently, and Hardy intoned: "Greg Milton, I'm arresting you for the murders of Dorothy Vine and Kevin Tyler... You have the right to remain silent when questioned, but what you fail to disclose cannot be used for your defence, and anything you do say can be used against you in a court of law."

Constable Hardy sounded either as if he'd never done this before, or was not quite sure that he was doing the right thing... or both. At any rate, Daisy made straight for where he was standing, aiming for the sound of his voice, and reached out to touch him with her hand as soon as she was within range. The uniformed bobbies around him stepped out of her way, as she knew they would.

"Constable! What is this? It can't be true! Mister Milton has a valid alibi for both murders, as you well know... or has something entirely unexpected come to light? And if you're

141

arresting him for Thea's murder, then may I conclude that her dead body has been found at last?"

"Ah... erm... hello there Mrs Hayes. I'm afraid I'm not at liberty to give you any information... ongoing investigation and all that."

"Well, as it happens, there are other things we're not supposed to disclose, you and me, but I'm starting to wonder about the wisdom of that! The man I'm referring to will have to face the music after all, if this is going to be the consequence of our discretion."

"Why... yes... I was having some doubts myself, Mrs Hayes, but it's not that simple... it's a bit too late to turn the boat around, if you know what I mean."

"In that case I will have to go and talk to your boss... once again. DCI Gilford is not here, is he? He sent out some underlings to do the dirty work for him? Then I'll have to go over to Horsham myself and reveal some unpalatable truths about a certain colleague of yours."

"Well... that's the thing, Madam. My, erm, colleague has persuaded the Chief that Quincy's... or Milton's alibis are not valid. 'You can't believe a *word* that man says', he told him. I heard it myself, as my desk is quite close to his."

DC Hardy now took Daisy by the elbow and led her into a quiet corner of the vast room. There he bent close to her ear and reported what Mundie had said. He'd told the chief that Quincy had gone to The Fly and Fish *already on the first night of the convention*, that he'd spent a fortune buying rounds for everybody, and then asked the regulars to cover for him the next night. Then Mundie had implied that the same thing *might* have happened for the second alibi as well.

"Wonderful!" Daisy muttered.

"When I heard him telling such lies, Mrs Hayes, I didn't dare to speak up, and you know why? Because I could see that the Chief was *lapping it up*. He believed the whole story, hook, line, and sinker."

"What do you expect, Hardy? There's no better way of lying than to tell people what they want to hear."

— 2 —

"This won't do at all, Chief Inspector," Daisy hissed as she sat down in front of him in his glass cubicle. Hardy had just escorted her to a chair, all too happy to let her set things straight with his boss; it was Darren who'd driven her over to the CID headquarter, almost tailing the police cars bringing in poor Quincy.

"Mrs Hayes, DC Hardy gave me to understand that you have some important information to impart urgently... Well, what is it now? I'm all ears."

"I don't know what has gotten into you, sir, but you've just arrested the wrong man! This won't do at all. I happen to know exactly who killed Thea, and who killed Jack Reaper, and the very idea that one person killed them both is ridiculous."

"Not at all. If you admit that Mr Quincy's alibis are shaky—and I have valid reasons to assume that they are—then you can also question his story about seeing Reaper driving away with Mrs Slayer in the passenger seat that night. I'm assuming they were both murdered by the same suspect, *at another time.*"

Oh! that Mundie has a lot to answer for, Daisy thought, seething.

"Well I find that a bit rich! Since when does a shaky alibi automatically make someone guilty as charged? Besides, I spoke to Ruth Vine only this morning about Quincy's alibi for the night that we know for a *fact* is the one when Reaper was killed, and she confirmed it. And I'll grant you that

Quincy had a strong motive to murder the man, but when I challenged him about that, none too subtly, believe me, he answered very reasonably that after spending fifteen years behind bars he knew better than to seek revenge by killing someone..."

He'd even quoted the Bible at her, but Daisy didn't say this to the inspector. It was something from Proverbs about people who ambush themselves and lie in wait for their own destruction. In other words, the former jailbird was enjoying himself immensely just watching his old enemy getting what was coming to him... from someone else.

"And what's more," Daisy went on after catching her breath again, "although Quincy had every reason to kill Jack Reaper, he had none at all to *slaughter* Mrs Slayer. Because that's what your men have discovered, isn't it? They found her dead body near a lake, maybe in the water or in the boot of Reaper's Jaguar, and perhaps the car had been dumped in that lake as well..."

Gilford wanted to protest again but the irritating old busybody raised her hand peremptorily to stop him: "You're not at liberty to tell, I'm aware of that, but it doesn't mean that I don't know what happened. I can easily imagine. The police surgeon who examined her remains concluded that her head had been bashed in with a heavy, blunt object, am I right? Major trauma to the skull, multiple fractures causing instantaneous death, and not a *trace* of water in her lungs if her body was fished out of the drink."

"Yes, well, you were right about Mrs Slayer's fate and about where we could find her body, I'll give you that. But it's the *time* of death I'm not so sure about... However, we have to leave that aspect of the investigation to others, and therefore we're not going to get definitive answers any time soon. It's quite galling when you stop to think about it: my men had no choice but to call in the Surrey colleagues and

144

those from the Met after they found the body, and let them take over the case."

"Well at least it's the West Sussex CID who handed the corpse to them on a silver platter, you could say, and that also counts for something."

Daisy reflected that this was probably the main reason why Gilford had rushed into arresting poor Quincy: to take back the initiative and stay ahead of the competition. Time to be diplomatic about the man's foibles.

"Listen, Inspector, I understand your frustrations, believe me, but is it wise to arrest a suspect even before the results of the post-mortem have come in? You may have to release him again if those results are not what you're expecting."

"It's my privilege to hold a suspect in custody for twenty-four hours before I decide to bring him before a judge, or to release him. I'm afraid Mr Milton is going to spend the night behind bars once again, and in the meantime we're going to grill him thoroughly, you can count on that!"

So much for diplomacy.

"Wonderful! I know that I won't be able to change your mind right now, but I want to give you a warning all the same. Greg Milton is *not* going to be unjustly accused again if I have anything to say about it, do you understand? He's not going to spend the rest of his life behind bars for a crime he couldn't *possibly* have committed... I already told you, I know exactly what happened, and if necessary I will share that knowledge with anyone who can help me to clear his name... If it should ever come to a trial, God forbid, that will include the counsel for the defence, and believe me, with what I can tell them they'll have their work cut out for them."

Gilford didn't answer anything to this tirade, but he didn't fly off the handle nor put an end to the interview either. Daisy realised that he must be rather shaken by what she'd just said, he appeared to be sulking, a bit, but didn't dare to dismiss her out of hand. Time to press her advantage. Very softly she started speaking again, very gently.

"Inspector, the best thing you can do is to help me unmask the *real* killer, the one who murdered Jack Reaper. But we still need some testimony from a few witnesses, and to uncover a missing piece of evidence, so a few arrangements need to be made..."

The Chief started stirring in his seat and rasped his throat tentatively. He was listening, and Daisy went on: "Now, the case is quite complicated, and it seems to me that the best way to sort it out is to stage a 'big reveal scene', you know, Hercule Poirot style, in the library at Bottomleigh House. There, in the presence of all the people involved in the case, I could summarize the sequence of events, present the clues one by one and elucidate the red herrings that almost led us astray, so that the ins and outs of the case will finally become crystal clear. Then you, Inspector, will be able to personally arrest one of the two murderers, the one that is still alive... What do you think, wouldn't that be something?"

DCI Gilford didn't say no to that.

— 3 —

Once again, in the early afternoon of the next day, many guests arrived at the Manor Hotel. Not incidentally it was the last day of the Murder Convention, that is to say it had initially been planned that the participants would go home the following morning.

The first car that scrunched to a halt on the gravel of the drive came all the way from London, and when DI Collins emerged from it with a few colleagues from the Metropolitan CID, Daisy was there in the colonnaded portico, already waiting to welcome him with Darren and Beatrice by her side.

146

"Mrs Hayes!" he exclaimed, "why do I feel like I wasted my breath when I asked you to refrain from any further enquiries?"

"Don't blame me, Inspector, I'm afraid DCI Gilford has claimed back an investigation that is his by rights... and I'm merely assisting, to the best of my abilities."

"Assisting, eh? I'm looking forward to that!"

Other cars arrived in rapid succession, a few publishers from London, some police brass from Surrey, the local coroner, crown prosecutor, and Division Commissioner. Daisy welcomed them all as if it were something she did every day: "Please, take a seat in the library, the doors are wide open on the other side of the entrance hall, straight ahead."

In the said library the reading tables had been moved aside and pushed against the walls; the sofas and armchairs had been set up in a wide circle, with chairs from the dining room being carried in to complete the numbers. Members of the staff were still busy with these arrangements under Sondra's direction; big thermos cans with coffee and tea at the ready on one of the side tables. For this was going to be a public hearing in front of a large audience, Daisy wanted it so and the coroner had agreed. The writers would be there, obviously, they would be coming down at any moment, and the two who'd played truant were expected to come back as well. Daisy had even invited the staff to attend, to the great dissatisfaction of their employer, who grumbled that this was not the kind of business his workers were being paid for, "If I may say so."

"The proceedings won't last much longer than an hour, an hour and a half at most, so please have a heart, Robbins, and think about the free publicity your hotel will be getting when we're done. The story will be all over the front pages, nationwide, I can tell you that much."

"Yes, but my establishment will now be associated with

murder!"

"The excitement will be all the greater. Mark my words, there's no such thing as bad publicity, nothing beats a spectacular crime to draw the crowds."

Finally the delegation from Horsham arrived in big numbers, with many cars. They seemed to have left only a skeleton staff behind at their headquarters. When Gilford greeted Daisy, the first thing she asked was, "Did you bring poor Quincy with you? Quincy! Are you all right?"

"Yes, I'm over here my dear, and I'm doing fine. Thank you for asking."

The Chief was rather miffed by this outburst of concern for his prisoner, and asked stiffly, "Has everyone arrived yet, Mrs Hayes? Shall we proceed?"

"Yes, yes, I believe everything is ready."

And they all went inside.

As they entered the vast room, the expectant hum that greeted them reminded Daisy of those long-bygone days when she and Ralph's gang had performed an absurd little play for the assembled household, guests, and staff: 'Murder of a Corpse'. But that had been in the attic instead of the library. And this time she would mostly be delivering a long monologue on her own. But there was nothing to be nervous about, she told herself, for she knew exactly what she wanted to say.

First the local coroner briefly took the floor, and announced rather formally that this was to be an informal affair, "In the line of an inquest hearing, you understand, but without any legal basis. All the usual procedures and their attendant paperwork will be taken care of at a later stage... Mrs Hayes, you have my blessing, and you may proceed. The floor is all yours."

So Daisy stepped forward, with Darren wheeling himself into position right next to her. "Who do you want to talk to first?"

"The coroner, and Gilford."

"Okay, they're sitting next to one another in front of you, at eleven o'clock."

"Great. Thanks."

Daisy adjusted her position slightly to the left, and Darren turned his chair a bit so that he too was facing them straight. This was how he would be communicating the position of different people sitting in a large circle all around them, when needed.

"Coroner, thank you for allowing me to lead this brief, informal inquest," Daisy started, "and you, DCI Gilford, many thanks for helping me with some last-minute preparations. The affair that brings us together here today started all the way back in 1980, with an abduction and blackmail case that caused quite a sensation at the time. Maybe some of you remember it."

She explained that the important thing to keep in mind was that Theodora Slayer had been writing a novel based on the 'Bowen case', as it was called, when she'd arrived at the hotel on the first day of the Murder Convention. And the dramatic events that followed all derived from that fact.

"Now, Mr Alexander..."

"He's sitting at three o'clock," Darren whispered while Daisy turned to the right, "and Beatrice is sitting right next to her darling Pee-Wee."

"...Mr Alexander, you're the one who told me about 'Tables Turned in Hell', the new novel, and you'll be able to testify to the police about its plot, as far as it is known to you... and they will need a copy of the ten pages that are still in your possession."

"No problem, Mrs Hayes, I'm at their disposal."

"But that is for later. For the moment we only need to know that Mrs Slayer had imagined that the kidnapping in

1980 had been a *staged* affair, a setup, and that an innocent man had been framed for it and sent to jail, while the real perpetrator pocketed the ransom money. This story was made up by her, but what she was writing happened to be quite close to the truth."

The real perpetrator in the Bowen affair, if you followed this scenario, was none other than Jack Reaper, who'd been invited to the Murder Convention for the first time. Mrs Slayer didn't know that this new member of the Top Ten Club was really Kevin Tyler, the detective who'd arrested the abductor and saved the kidnapped girl. In fact, Daisy remarked, almost no one had recognized him, which led her to the conclusion that he must have looked different from fifteen years before, somehow, maybe sporting a beard, or on the contrary being newly clean-shaven... That was for the sighted investigators to determine.

"Nevertheless, Kevin Tyler, or Jack Reaper, somehow found out that Thea was writing a novel about him, and that she'd come uncomfortably close to the truth. He must have overheard her discussing the project with Lee Quincy, who was also involved in the Bowen case. His real name is Greg Milton, he's the man who was put behind bars by Detective Tyler, and who inspired the plot of Tables Turned in Hell... Thea had invited him precisely to hear his side of the story and discuss the plot of her novel with him. And this brings us straight to the 'night of the scream'.

"Jack Reaper decided to act at once and to destroy the manuscript in the middle of the night, when he could do it unseen. He'd probably figured out that there was only one typescript in existence, and concluded that destroying it would be such a blow that it was likely to make Thea Slayer drop the project entirely. It must not have been too hard for him to get his hands on it, for the Murder Convention turned out to be rather relaxed, the participants popping in and out of one another's rooms freely. No one thought of locking their door, I noticed this informal atmosphere myself."

Daisy now invited her audience to *imagine* how Jack Reaper slunk down to the library in the middle of the night, proceeded to relight the fire in the hearth, then ripped the typescript to pieces and started feeding fistfuls of paper snippets to the flames. Probably he'd decided to burn it on the spur of the moment that night, without a thought for the possible consequences. Surely he didn't have murder on his mind...

Meanwhile Theodora Slayer woke up in her room, plagued by a strong urge to make a small change in her work-in-progress, a normal thing at this stage, and discovered that her manuscript had gone missing. After searching her room for a while, to no avail, she decided to go down to the library and have a look there, for she could have left it behind after her last brainstorming session with Quincy... and that is when she caught Jack Reaper in the act of burning it.

"She must have rushed forward to stop him, but it was too late, her precious manuscript had already been reduced to ashes. And while she hissed and sputtered, completely bewildered by this wanton act of destruction, she must have realized who Jack Reaper really was. This was the moment when she put two and two together, and perhaps remembered the pictures from the press reports fifteen years before. 'It's *you*,' she cried, 'you're the *real* kidnapper! I should have known!'

"And that was when Jack Reaper realized that his cover had been blown. The game was over. Theodora Slayer had uncovered the truth. From that moment on she could only expose him, and this would inevitably lead to his downfall and to retribution. He needed to stop her. He had to shut her up. He seized one of the heavy silver candlesticks standing on the mantelpiece and advanced on the elderly lady, raising it with murderous intent in his eyes, as the saying goes.

"She retreated to the middle of the room, walking backwards, perhaps, bumping into the furniture, and in an ultimate attempt to stop him she cried out, 'I changed the names! I changed the names!' I have a witness who heard her utter these words, although he didn't really catch their meaning at the time, but more about that in a moment."

Daisy then described what happened next. The police surgeon's report had only just confirmed that the victim had died instantly from a heavy blow with a blunt object on her *forehead*. She had been facing her attacker at the moment of the fatal blow. "Traces of Theodora's blood could still be identified on the candlestick that we found in the pond the day before yesterday, right here on the premises. And the blood splatters on the rug were hers as well, but that had already been established at a much earlier stage of the investigation.

"So now you had a murder on the spur of the moment, and a murderer who was anxious to get rid of the body. Immediately he thought of enlisting the help of an accomplice, for there was one other member of the Top Ten Club that he thought he could trust completely, even to help him hide a murder. He went upstairs at once, woke up that person without a sound, and came down with *her* again a moment later. She helped him carry the body to his car and to load it into the front passenger seat. Jack Reaper must have carried the candlestick under his arm all the while, and he hurled it into the pond without thinking. Finally his accomplice helped him to push the jaguar down the slight incline so it would roll to the gate by the main road in complete silence... Now, where is Mister Kumar? I've personally invited him here today."

"At six o'clock, right behind you," Darren muttered, and his wife turned around. The people in the audience thought it quite a stunt, the way this blind sleuth managed to address people all around her directly, with a little help from her handsome partner.

"I'm here, Mrs Hayes," the night porter volunteered apprehensively. Had the moment come to confess that he'd dozed off that night?

"My dear Mister Kumar, you didn't notice much of these events, people sneaking up and down the stairs and slipping in and out of the library, and that is for the simple reason that you were sitting at the reception desk, monitoring the front door, while the library and the main staircase were situated behind your back... Nevertheless, you're an essential witness, because you heard Mrs Slayer exclaiming twice: 'I changed the names!' Only, you couldn't tell *where* exactly those words came from within the vast gloomy building around you; they could have come from upstairs as well."

And then there was another essential piece of information that she'd received from Mister Kumar, Daisy explained. The famous scream could never have been produced by old Mrs Slayer, who had a rather deep and hoarse voice, but it had sounded much younger, and had the range and *tessitura* of a natural soprano.

"You have to understand that Mister Kumar is probably the person who heard the scream at closest range that night. Then only yesterday he was present too at my informal little birthday party, at my special invitation again, and he could confirm that one person in particular did indeed sing along with the others in such a voice: *Miss Maple.*"

Now Daisy heard some hissing and tutting from her right-hand side. "At three o'clock again," Darren whispered, and his wife turned to face the young mystery writer just as she scoffed, "That doesn't prove a thing!" But out of nervousness she uttered these words in a girlish, squeaky way that only confirmed Daisy's assertion. She rasped her throat to cover her embarrassment.

"I'm aware of that," Daisy said levelly, "and I have to admit that I didn't hear 'the scream' myself, but the point I'm trying to make is this: you're the one who helped Jack Reaper to carry Theodora's body to his car, and just before the two of you left the library through the French windows, you contributed a finishing touch of your own. You screamed at the top of your lungs, long and hard."

It was a clever ploy, Daisy explained, improvised on the spur of the moment, based on the counterintuitive insight that instead of keeping quiet, rousing the whole place at once would lead to a great deal more confusion.

"We'll soon find out that confusion is your speciality, Miss Maple."

While the mystery writers came downstairs to find out what was going on and gathered by the library door, at the back of the building, she and Jack Reaper were plodding to the car park at the side of it, out of sight and out of hearing, with the dead body between them. After the killer had silently rolled away in his Jaguar, his clever helper tiptoed back to the foot of the terrace wall, knocked in a pane of a basement window and gained entry to the building again. The basement was connected to the rest of the house by the old backstairs that the servants had used when the kitchens, pantries, and laundries had still been situated 'downstairs'. Aggie Maple went back to her room, and only moments later she descended the main stairs and joined the others.

"Now, the experts among you, I mean the *real* police officers and such, will perhaps be thinking that all this is pure conjecture on my part, and they'll be right, I'm aware of that. But there are *two* essential elements in this whole affair that are proven facts already at this stage. A manuscript was burned in the library's fireplace, and the only fragment that survived the flames was identified by the victim's publisher.

154

Secondly, the victim's autopsy revealed a blow on the head as the cause of death, and her blood was found on the rug and on the candlestick... There's still a lot of work to be done on the case, but I think it's safe to conclude that Theodora Slayer was really murdered by Jack Reaper, and that the reconstruction I've just proposed cannot be far from the truth."

There was a rumble of approval from the public in the room, but it was impossible to say if it originated from the police officers as well. Daisy swallowed hard, her mouth felt dry and she regretted not having something to drink at her disposal. A few sips would have been welcome at that moment. Darren noticed her hand going up to her throat in an unconscious gesture, and he motioned one of the kitchen helpers at the drinks table to bring over something for his wife, tipping an imaginary beaker in front of his mouth. "Take a breath, sweetness, here comes a drink for you."

So after a pause and a drink of water, Daisy resumed her presentation.

"Ladies and gentlemen, the question that still needs to be answered now, is who murdered Mrs Slayer's killer a few nights later. Jack Reaper was strangled from behind with a cord, probably an electric cord, and the time of death has been established by the usual and officially sanctioned methods. The reality of the crime and its timing are not in doubt. What is still open to discussion, however, is the identity of the killer."

With a little help from Darren once more, she turned to face the quarter of the circle where the prisoner was sitting between two watchful policemen.

"Mister Quincy... or must I call you Greg Milton?"

"I answer to both names with equal pride, Mrs Hayes."

"And right you are. You've achieved something remarkable as Lee Quincy, and as Greg Milton your name was unjustly sullied, as far as I can make out... I hope you're not manacled, right now?"

"No, DC Hardy took the manacles off when we entered the room... like you asked him to."

"Good! Now, please tell us what happened on the day you arrived here, at the start of the Murder Convention. I suppose you recognized Jack Reaper at once?"

"Yes, and he recognized me, I could tell, but we both didn't let on and shook hands like fellow-authors who meet for the first time."

"But it must have been a shock! Did you start plotting your revenge at once?"

"It was a shock all right, but there was no call to start plotting anything at that moment. First because I've had plenty of time to do that in jail, and after all these years the revenge fantasies have paled, I can assure you. The fact that I wrote seven novels demonstrates that I've unburdened my mind well enough... But more importantly, Theodora's pet project looked like it was going to provide plenty of satisfaction in that respect."

"But you didn't tell her who Jack Reaper really was?"

"Not me, no. I was afraid it would be too much of a distraction from our project if she heard the truth, so I let it rest."

"All right."

Daisy now explained that for a short while after Kevin Tyler was found dead in a forest cottage in Surrey, Lee Quincy, or Greg Milton, had been considered as a prime suspect. He knew about the existence of the cottage and could have remembered its location, for the simple reason that he'd been arrested there by the victim himself fifteen years before. When he'd spotted him driving north with Mrs Slayer's corpse, during 'the night of the scream', he could easily have concluded that his enemy would seek refuge there, and would be particularly vulnerable. Ideal circumstances for revenge.

"But there wasn't any evidence that could *prove* Mr Milton's presence on the crime scene. On the contrary, it soon became clear that he had a valid alibi—if you disregarded certain police cock-ups—and that the car that had left its tire marks on the crime scene was none other than Thea's own Bentley... and that is when I understood who Tyler's killer really was."

Daisy turned back to face Aggie Maple again, because she knew that the youngest author of the club was sitting right next to her publisher, Mr Fisher, from Scribblers & Sons. Darren had 'clocked' the man when he'd arrived and introduced himself to the Chief, and he'd informed his wife.

She now said, "Mr Fisher, I recently heard from one of your star authors, Mr Jim Cross, that Miss Agatha Maple is also one of your firm's authors. That name is obviously a pseudonym as well, just like Jack Reaper, so what can you tell us about her true identity? The police is going to interrogate you under caution about this soon enough, and then you'll have to testify under oath before a court of law, whereupon it will become public knowledge anyway. So you might as well tell us the truth right now."

Confronted with such a verbal onslaught, the man didn't have much choice but to capitulate at once, and he told the assembled audience that Agatha Maple's real name was *Tilly Bowen*... And yes, she was a protégée of Jack Reaper's, who'd recommended her to their publishing house, and they'd never had any reason to regret taking her on as an author.

The squeaky voice they'd heard before piped up again, coming from the same spot where her publisher was sitting: "That's not fair! What has *that* got to do with anything?"

"Yes, Miss Maple, on the face of it you're just the poor young girl that was kidnapped by Greg Milton in 1980, and the friendly detective who freed you from your dire predicament gave you a leg-up to become a successful mystery writer just like himself. So there are no grounds to suspect you of killing him... on the contrary. But although you helped Jack Reaper dispose of Thea Slayer's body that night, you were also angry at him. He was jeopardizing the dangerous secrets the two of you shared, for no good reason at all, except that he'd panicked and wasn't able to control his violent impulses."

"What on earth are you *talking* about, you crazy blind woman?"

Daisy ignored this outburst and turned to where Gilford was sitting, not far from Lee Quincy.

"Chief inspector, have you any news from Mundie and his men?"

"Not yet, Mrs Hayes, I'm sending someone upstairs this instant to check what's taking them so long."

Then she addressed the prisoner again. "Please tell me something, Mr Quincy: when you arrived here on the first day of the Murder Convention and you were introduced to Agatha Maple, did you recognize Aggie Maple as well? Were you aware of her real identity?"

"No, actually I had never met her before, because as a sixteen-year-old girl, Tilly Bowen was not allowed to be present at my trial, even though her testimony was instrumental in my conviction."

"All right. I just wanted to make sure."

Daisy now turned to where the coroner and the police brass were sitting, so that she officially addressed the assembled public as a whole again. She explained that she now wanted to give them another *reconstruction*, based on *conjecture*, of what had happened on the night Kevin Tyler had been killed.

First, it was clear that if Miss Maple had assisted her accomplice, Jack Reaper, to get rid of Mrs Slayer's body, she would have had the keys of the Bentley, because she could have searched for them on her person or in her room afterwards. Secondly, she could get away in the dark undetected, whenever she wanted, in the same way she'd reappeared unnoticed on the night of the scream: by way of the backstairs and through the cellars, then pushing the car downhill and starting the engine only at the end of the drive.

She must have arranged with Jack Reaper to bring him some supplies in his hideout as soon as the coast would be clear, and when she turned up at the hut in the woods he was waiting for her eagerly. The last thing he'd expected after welcoming her inside the cottage was that his accomplice would attack him from behind. Maybe he was expecting a hug, or a soothing massage of his neck and shoulders, instead of which she throttled him.

When she returned to the hotel, Mister Kumar was on duty, and he thought he heard *two* cars arriving in the middle of the night, almost at the same time, but when Mister Quincy and Miss Vine came inside, he'd assumed that each of them had come home in their own car. However, Aggie had probably driven up right behind them with her headlights off to conceal her arrival, so that Mister Quincy and Miss Vine, sharing the same car, didn't notice she was tailing them. Again she entered through a basement window and went up to her room by way of the backstairs.

"This is ridiculous!" Aggie cried, "you have no evidence whatsoever against me. Nobody has. The story you just made up is *outrageous*, preposterous!"

"But is it, really?" Daisy asked, turning back to her, "I've been wondering; I've been thinking things over a lot lately; I've been racking my brains about your role in this whole plot, you know.

"Thinking back to the Bowen case in 1980, I can imagine

159

a cop who is corrupt and bold enough to come up with such a scheme. But how on earth would he have been able to enlist the complicity of the sixteen-year-old daughter of a wealthy man to carry out the plot? He needed her to lie to the police consistently, for hours on end, without faltering even once. Could she be trusted to pull that off, and why would she want to do that for him?

"No, it is much more logical to conclude that it's the rich girl who recruited the cop. That was also much easier for her to do, she only needed to hang out in the usual haunts of unattached young police detectives: nightclubs or discos that could easily be identified if you got down to it. That is where Tilly Bowen got in touch with Kevin Tyler, that is when she *seduced* him into going along with her scheme to extort a substantial ransom from her father. She was the mastermind from the start, he only agreed with her plans for the money, or perhaps because he was quite smitten with such a sexy young thing.

"At any rate you both must have felt that Thea Slayer was getting dangerously close to the truth with the story of *Mildred* she'd made up, and was about to publish."

Daisy fell silent after these words, she had now said all she wanted to say, and it was time to move on to the last act of the drama. The audience felt that something portentous was about to happen, and everyone seemed to hold their breath. Right on cue a couple of men entered the library, producing some fumbling noises by the door, and DS Mundie called out in an untypically guilty-sounding way: "Guvnor! You wanted me to report?"

Daisy had never been so happy to hear his voice, but then he added: "We haven't found anything so far!" and her heart sank.

"Are you sure?" Gilford stammered, "you must keep searching!"

"That's what my men are doing, Sir, but it's not looking good. There aren't that many hiding places in a hotel room, you know."

"Did you look in the bathroom? The toilet siphon? Inside the tank?"

"That's the *first* place we checked out!"

During this exchange Daisy bent over Darren and asked in a whisper: "Does Aggie have a *handbag?*"

"Sure... never goes anywhere without it. It's almost as big as yours."

"Great! Thanks."

She raised herself again and called out: "Excuse me, Chief Inspector, may I ask: the search warrant you obtained, surely it also applies for a person's handbag?"

"Why... yes... it certainly does."

"Then I suggest that you go through the contents of Miss Maple's bag at once."

There were more fumbling sounds as a couple of uniforms wrestled with the young woman to pry her bag from her hands. "This is *private!*" she squeaked, "you have no right!" But to no avail. She had to let go, Gilford repeated that he had a search warrant, and Daisy could hear the characteristic rumbling and jangling sounds produced by someone vigorously pawing through the jumbled contents of a lady's cavernous leather purse.

"Ah, here we have them, Chief!" one of the policemen cried, and he held up a twinkling keyring. Everyone could see the capital B emblem enamelled on a metal badge fixed to it.

"The Bentley's keys!" Darren announced to Daisy.

"Thank God!"

"It doesn't prove a thing!" Aggie screamed, "Thea gave me those keys on the first day, because I told her I'd like to drive a Bentley just once in my life."

161

"That's no excuse," Daisy retorted at once, "you're still the only one who could have used the Bentley to drive to the hut in the woods."

But already Gilford had given the nod to DC Hardy, who approached the fresh suspect and intoned, "Miss Tilly Bowen, I'm arresting you for the murder of Kevin Tyler, and for other possible felonies to be determined at a later stage..."

This time the constable sounded very sure of himself.

The whole room remained silent at first, watching the culprit being led away by Hardy and two uniformed men, she shaking them off when they tried to hold her elbows left and right. Nevertheless Aggie Maple had no choice but to follow them out of the library without another word, frowning fiercely. As soon as the little group had left, the other people present started commenting among themselves, marvelling at the unexpected turn the events had taken, producing an excited hum of hushed conversations. Daisy remained in the middle of the room, standing by Darren's side, smiling, and before anyone else could come forward to congratulate her, Gilford stepped over in a few lanky strides and said, "My dear Mrs Hayes, what did you mean a while back with your remark that *certain* police cock-ups should be disregarded?"

"Did I say that? Well, I don't know, but maybe you shouldn't take everything DS Mundie tells you at face value. That man sometimes seems to have an agenda of his own... Which reminds me: did anyone take down my explanations just now? I'm afraid it was a rather complicated story, and we don't want any more muddles, do we?"

"No worries, Madam, constable Hardy was taking notes all the time."

"Oh, good. Excellent!"

The Chief hurried away when he noticed his colleague from Scotland Yard right behind him, apparently eager to speak to the heroine of the moment in his turn. Collins seized

Daisy's hand and said warmly, "I can't tell you how impressed I am, Mrs Hayes. You really did it this time: you managed to solve the case singlehandedly."

"Why, thank you, Detective Inspector... So you're not angry at me?"

"Not in the least!"

Then Beatrice was hugging her childhood friend, her odour and her usual perfume utterly familiar to Daisy, and she mumbled in her ear, "What does he mean: 'this time'? You do it *every* time!"

"Yes, but Collins isn't aware of that."

Finally Bee's old chum, Rupert Alexander, pumped Daisy's hand enthusiastically and repeated his offer to take her on as an author.

"When I was listening to your brilliant exposition, my dear, so concise and clear, I kept thinking what an outstanding mystery writer you would make."

"That's very kind of you, sir, but I don't believe I could ever *make up* a story like that, you know. Darren and I are only good at sorting the facts from the foibles, and at envisioning what *really* happened."

THE END

A note on the author

Nick Aaron is Dutch, but he was born in South Africa (1956), where he attended a British-style boarding school, in Pietersburg, Transvaal. Later he lived in Lausanne (Switzerland), in Rotterdam, Luxembourg and Belgium. He worked for the European Parliament as a printer and proofreader. Currently he's retired and lives in Malines.

Recently, after writing in Dutch and French for many years, the author went back to the language of his mid-century South African childhood. A potential global readership was the incentive; the trigger was the character of Daisy Hayes, who asserted herself in his mind wholly formed.

Author's homepage: www.nickaaronauthor.com

BV - #0069 - 140125 - C0 - 203/133/12 - PB - 9789083433837 - Gloss Lamination